Real Mothers

Real Mothers

Vivian Sihshu Yenika

iUniverse, Inc.
New York Lincoln Shanghai

Real Mothers

iUniverse books may be ordered through booksellers or by contacting:

iUniverse
2021 Pine Lake Road, Suite 100
Lincoln, NE 68512
www.iuniverse.com
1-800-Authors (1-800-288-4677)

ISBN-13: 978-0-595-38266-8 (pbk)
ISBN-13: 978-0-595-82637-7 (ebk)
ISBN-10: 0-595-38266-5 (pbk)
ISBN-10: 0-595-82637-7 (ebk)

Printed in the United States of America

To the Memory of My Father, Mathias Bayena Yenika, with love

and

You too, Bayenique, with lots of love

Prologue

Early one morning in the month of August when there was a heavy down pour of rain, and lightning crisscrossing the heavenly skies at odd moments, a figure was seen ascending the small hill that bridged Kake and Mbonge road. It kept raining as thunder rumbled across the skies, pausing every now and then to observe the scene beneath it—to stare at the water pouring over this desolate person as he swaggered along a segment of road that still had some tar. He was completely drenched but kept staggering on as though it was a bright and sunny day. There were moments that he would pause to let a truck drive past him. It would speed along bouncing from one pothole to another as it splashed slush all over this wretched, young fellow. But the child didn't mind. He didn't bother to wipe the dirt off his body, for the heavy raindrops did a better job at that. Then another vehicle would splash more and more, and sometimes the driver would put his head out to spit insults at him. He was a mad man, one driver would say; a vagabond, another would shout at the top of his voice; a lunatic! Each would say this and speed up the steep hill on their way to the heart of Kumba town.

Their insults didn't bother this man-child. Why should he complain when he had looked for it? Had he not asked for it? If he had not been walking out there where would they have had the opportunity to rid their systems of these insults? Or the chance to splash mud on him?

The white T-shirt his mother had bought for him a long time ago clung fervently to his wet, skinny body; only it was no longer white. It was now tan in color and had isolated spots that had the look of unbrewed dark coffee. An old sweater that used to be the best thing in his closet hung heavily on his right arm as he constantly struggled to pull his droopy trousers up. It was hard to imagine that only twelve months ago this same pair of trousers had fitted him so well—and there had been moments when he had been afraid that it would be too tight! The toes of his right foot stuck out of the dark, torn, muddy shoes he was wearing, a pair of canvas that used to be white. On his head, he had a faded yellow cap with a scrawling that resembled the words PAMOL only the "L" was missing the bottom curve, and the "O" now looked like a "C."

He kept adjusting the cap on his head as he trod on braving the rain, the lightning, and the thunder that accompanied the wet, cold, heavy drops. He could feel these drops rinsing off the filth he had accumulated both from his eight hours nightmarish boat ride from Calabar, and the new dirt he had picked up from the vehicles that passed him on the way. The hard cold drops felt good on his body, even though he shivered from it all. It was better than being covered by the dark mud that at times made his body itch. He smiled at this thought, and for once since his departure from home he ventured to think he was lucky to be alive. Did he not have a place to which he could always flee back? A place where someone would take care of him in spite of everything! His lips twitched. Another smile, then he quickly knitted his eyebrow as another thought crossed his mind. He was the only one who knew what the problem was. Na so life dey.

As he finally reached the top of the steep hill, he stood on one spot for a few minutes and heaved a long sigh. Without hesitating he picked up some dirt from the side of the road and poured over his body. He took a step, paused and looked toward the direction he was coming from; then asked himself repeatedly why his life had really turned out this way. There was no answer to this question—he knew that, but couldn't help asking it. He searched for answers hard squinting to no avail. Satisfied the brain behind his broad forehead had no answer, he leaned forward and adjusted his shoelace before branching off to the street on his right. It was Krammer Street; the street where his mother's house has always been waiting and stood waiting…Now he put on his wet, heavy, cold, brown, sweater, and pulled his cap closer to his eyes before daring forward on the muddy road. A few steps forward he ran into several cars that were stuck in the six-inch dark, gluey mud they had danced into by the side of this unpaved road.

The engines screeched and moaned hours on end as the back tires rotated without moving the vehicles forward. One driver, frustrated at his futile attempts at getting the car out of the gutter he had accidentally spun into, got out and walked away. Minutes later, he reappeared with five boys from a roadside garage that made its profits from such emergencies. Armed with shovels and stones, they dug the ground beneath each tire, supported it with a huge piece of stone and propelled the car forward. They did this a couple of times and the car was soon out of there. The car owner gave them some money and drove off in the opposite direction without a backward glance. Three other car owners followed his example and left. But there was one who would not use the garage boys. This one who didn't hire the boys' services stayed behind and struggled on his own. With the driver's door opened he tried to push and steer the wheel at the same time, but the car would not budge. Then the car owner noticed this miserable person who kept tumbling on the slippery road. At first, he didn't want to solicit this youth's help, but then again he changed his mind and beckoned for the man-child to come. The boy hesitated for one brief moment then slowly approached the car owner. With the little strength left in his lanky body he pushed, but the car would not move an inch. He thought his rib cage would crack as he pushed harder and harder. But push he must. Why? He didn't know. One more shove and that was when he felt it. The pain was sharp and quick. At first, he thought he could brave it as he had done during this past year. But no. It came again, sudden and fast cutting across his abdomen. He grabbed the area and wandered off to the side of the road and vomited. The driver noticed this and got angry. "Where do you think you're going?"

The youth ignored him.

"Ah, say, where do you think you are going, you dis yam head?" the driver yelled after the stooped figure by the side of the road. The boy got up and returned to the car. He pushed one more time before slacking off again. This time the driver had had it.

"Don't you touch my car again, you…" he screamed.

The man-child obeyed. He made no more attempts to push the car out of there again. But he waited. He stood there and waited. The car owner sighed, "Okay, take something and buy bread before you break into two and start telling people that my car did it."

The man-child took the lone clean coin the car owner had offered him, but he remained standing by the car. "Is fifty francs not enough for bread?" the car owner asked, a little surprised. There was no answer from the wretched person he had just taken pity upon. "Get out of here before you make me dream!" he scoffed, "Bone, bone all over like someone who has suffered from cholera. Don't people eat where you come from?"

The man-child gazed past him. For a moment, he thought he was back where he was just coming from—that heavy masculine voice, that accent! It all sounded so close. "Hey, ah beg, make you go-oh before you come die here and start accusing me," the car owner finally appealed.

"Yes sah," the man-child retorted and headed in the direction he had been going before the interruption. He staggered toward the direction of his mother's house. As he walked on he attempted to put the coin in his back pocket, but each time it would slip through his shaky fingers and fall onto the muddy road. He would bend over to pick it, shivering all the way down and up as a biting cool draft landed on his slightly exposed waist, where the oversized trousers kept shifting.

When he finally got it in the pocket he moved on. He fell a few more times on this slippery road, and each time he would slowly pick himself up and plunge further into the heart of Krammer Street. At last, he spotted the house he had left barely twelve months ago. A faint smile appeared on the corner of his tight lips as he stood there in disbelief. He stood on the same spot, at an intersection for a couple of minutes and stared at his mother's house with fond memory. Tears glided down his cheeks. He could see the door wide open as always with the curtain tied halfway so rainwater splashing on the verandah wouldn't get it wet. There were aluminum buckets and basins lined out on the concrete verandah eagerly trapping the abundant natural water that sprinkled generously from above. With one last effort, this miserable man-child crossed over to the side of the road where the house stood waiting...A fragile looking plank house that had cracks, paint chips and tiny hollow spots on most sections of the four walls that supported it. The wooden window stood open and he could see a woman's plaited hair. He chuckled. That must be Chinyere, he thought. It was just like her to lean against the windowsill each time she was trying to make her point. Then he heard, "You shut up there with your kwacoco head!" That must be Sister Glory, he thought. It was just like her to bark at people. This thought was still going on in his mind when someone pushed the tied curtain aside, and a young woman slowly walked her way on to the damp verandah. He noticed her protruding stomach, then his eyes landed on her unsmiling face, and for a brief moment he gasped for breath as his legs suddenly went limb. He stood there and just gazed speechlessly at this woman.

She stood on the verandah with both hands supporting her tired waist as she sniffed the fresh evening air. Then she looked around her and sighed. "Ay say-eh, Simon, who do you think is going to pour this water into the drum?" she snapped in her usual fashion. But before the person she was addressing could reply, she carried on, "Not me with my belly. I know you all will be happy if I miscarry now, but I won't! And it is twin this time. You can all eat your heads out!" She opened her mouth to say more but left it gaping as her eyes landed on this dirty looking, emaciated man-child that was watching her from the corner of the street. "My Mami-eh! Sister-oh! You people should come at once. Die man don wake up from grave." She moved a step closer then stepped back to lean against the front door.

"They suffered you? Tell me what happened."

"Glory," a solemn voice called from behind her, "Let this not be a joke or else I will make you have that your child now."

"No, Sister, just come and see for yourself."

Everyone in the parlor rushed out in spite of the rain. Monday remained standing where he was, and like the man he had been trying to be he would not break down yet for all to see.

"Monday? Is that really you? Monday! Eh? My child, is it really you? Weh, child, what happened? What did they do to you? Weh, my suffer pickin!" At this, their mother burst into tears as the apparition wobbled toward them.

"My child, what happened to you so-eh? Come elay me...Don't mind my clean wrapper. Just come." She whimpered, embraced her son and dragged him indoor away from the eyes of the neighbors who had begun gathering with umbrellas over their heads as they anticipated a juicy story to spread around.

Noticing the crowd getting larger, Chinyere stormed out of the room. "I can't believe this!" she exclaimed, clapping her hands in shocking disbelief. "These people, don't they have shame? Don't you people have shame?" She posed this question to the crowd that had begun whispering excitedly. As she saw their lips beginning to move more and more, she took one stride outside the verandah where she was *really, really* closer to them and screamed, "Go to your Mama and Papa's house, you people with no shame! Haven't you seen a child returning home in your life? Eh?" She then slammed the door in their faces and sighed. Minutes later, she shut the windows too, but this didn't send the people away. They clambered around the verandah with some struggling to place their ears on the cracks around the plank walls and the windows in a desperate attempt to hear what was being discussed in the house. Sister Nkongho only too aware of this refrained from asking her son any more questions.

"Chinyere, go to the kitchen and make something for your brother to eat; Simon you warm water for his bath and after that you run to the market and get Jacob. Glory..." their mother began but was hushed down by her first child and daughter—the Mami to be. "E, e, Sister Nkongho, I'm not there. Don't just ask me to do anything. I'm tired of your children and their irresponsible behavior!"

"My daughter, listen, let me speak."

"No, Sister! If I had gone off like that, who would have taken care of all these your battalion?"

"Mami, ah beg, no vex. You are a mother too now. You should stand these things…Besides, I just wanted to find out if you have bought more material for the baby's clothes."

"Oh, that! Yes. I will bring them to you. Just wait here. But Sister, I'm through with you and your children." At that moment, their grandmother emerged from the bedroom, looking frail as the years had begun catching up with her despite the numerous change of birth dates on her birth certificate. "Epo, what is it?"

"Aunty, Monday has come back home," Sister Nkongho replied.

"Oh, Mr. Akpan didn't want him." she said this as a matter of fact, then found her way to the nearest chair.

"How can you say a thing like that, Aunty?"

"I just know"

"You don't know everything."

"Okay, but I know that you are my child!" She grinned. "Epo, tell your Monday we want him here! Tell him he is our child!"

"All right, Aunty."

"Weh, Epo, but why did he even go sef-eh?"

"How should I know, na?" the younger woman sighed.

"My daughter, don't mind. At least, he knows now that the salt he has is better than the sugar he would have had." Aunty paused. "Besides putting it in tea, what do we really do with that sugar sef-eh? A piece of luxury that can never be available to all!" She snorted. Both women clapped their hands in wonder, then cupped their mouths and waited. Perhaps for a miracle to change their fate!

Chapter 1

"Efeti, your own too much-oh!" Nkongho chided the little girl.
Glory smiled and bounced off, wriggling her buttocks. The older woman watched intensely then sighed. As her daughter's back disappeared from the hospital premises Nkongho turned around. That's when she noticed Papa Joe gaping at the little girl. His eyes narrowed and a grin suddenly appeared on his face. Nkongho had seen enough.
"Not her, you dog!"
His eyes were still stuck on Glory's behind. Nkongho still in her white uniform stooped and gathered a handful of gravel and aimed blindly in his direction. He docked.
"You missed again!" He shouted laughing heartily before licking his lips several times poking his tongue out at the woman.
"Let me just catch you," Nkongho ventured as the remaining gravel in her hand trickled between her fingers.
"Joe, you dis man, my eyes are on you. Dog!"
He ignored her and disappeared into his outpatient office to resume duty. Nkongho sighed and returned to her own post in the female ward. She was one of two medical staff on duty that Saturday afternoon. But her mind, as usual was not on the job especially since Glory adopted a new style of walk pushing her buttocks backwards and twisting it slowly like a woman. Nkongho was tired of all the stares like the one Papa Joe always gave her daughter. All those eyes watching Glory's behind all the time with mouths salivating after her unripe daughter. She was just plain tired of it all. Those Volkswagens that stopped for her daughter day after day; those expensive gifts from Printania and worse yet, the five thousand

francs notes some have actually offered her oldest daughter. And Glory was still only in primary school!
No! Nkongho concluded one day. Enough was enough. She eventually informed her mother that Lobe Estate was extremely bad for her daughter. Bad men were everywhere. Bad managers who want to spoil her small girl before the child was even ready to be spoilt. And like that Nkongho handed in her resignation several months later. She packed her family of no one knows exactly how many and joined the medical staff at Kumba General hospital. She thought, at least in Kumba Glory would have some peace.

Her new living quarters was noticeably different from the two-room house she had in Camp 8 where she had spent the first ten years of her professional life. The house she rented was spacious—roomy enough for her battalion. That was all that mattered. And so her new life began in K Town in a house that was not built of bricks but a quartier she hoped would accommodate her and her children for a very long time—unless something happened. Just maybe! But where would a mother of children run to?

CHAPTER 2

"Ngozi, na your eyes dis? Ah, ah, how you forget us like this-eh?"
"Eh, eh, Sister Nkongho! When did you people come to our town, na?"
"About one month now."
"Then you never come find me? You know my shed, not so? Sister Nkongho, that Lobe like that, since Mr. Martin died and his Madam left that Lobe, it's hard for me to visit-oh."
"I know. He was a good man. Did you hear the news about him? They say his body didn't want to go back-oh. Hmm!"
"Sister, even if you were the one, would you let your die body leave the place where you have stayed all your life? Make dem leave the man in peace, ah! Aunty, how na? You still look like young girl," Ngozi complimented the older woman that stood by Sister Nkongho's side.
"I know, my daughter, but all this talking make my legs tire. Where be your shed?" Ngozi took them further into the market. Her shed stood in the heart of Kumba market, next to a cosmetic dealer's.
"Hmm!" Aunty exclaimed, "I didn't realize that your shed was this big."
Ngozi laughed. "Wait till you see Oga i own. It is two times my own." She continued laughing. "So which kind news na?"
"Oh, some people died; some made more children; some became big men and some like me tire the place." Nkongho replied nonchalantly.
"I know how you feel."
The two younger women locked eyes and burst out laughing.

Aunty sighed. "Ngozi, no mind am. You know our Glory is growing up and those managers." She shrugged her shoulders. "My daughter let me leave am so-oh."
"Aunty, are you telling me? Isn't that why my oga marry me quick, quick?"
Aunty grinned and followed Ngozi into the shed.
They both sat down to rest their legs.
"Sister, give me your list make I mark the things that you can get from my shed."
Nkongho gladly did. Ngozi crossed out half of the list.
"Now, these ones them so, I will show you where to get them. Na from my people." Ngozi took her to the different sheds and they picked up the stuff Nkongho wanted. When they returned, they added the others, which Ngozi had carefully set aside on the floor for them.
"I hear you have a battalion now in your house," Ngozi joked as she added some more items for Nkongho's children. Tears flooded Sister Nkongho's eyes. She picked up one of the baskets in the hook of her elbow as she cast a grateful glance at this child she had helped a long time ago when Ngozi had been found stranded on the Lobe beach. She smiled and then strolled away.

* * * *

The house Nkongho had rented for her family was big enough, or so she would like to think since it was the only house she could really afford for her thriving family. It was a plank house, not bricks like every other building around her. But it was built on solid concrete foundation. The landlord had told Nkongho and she believed him. She had to believe him in order to live there or else she would have to keep looking for a better place. Not that she could afford anything better even.

Actually, it wasn't quite up to five weeks since they had moved into town and they were still trying to settle down. They were trying hard to create space for each family member. No sooner had they sorted out this problem than for the neighbors to start paying their respects.

First, it was Mrs. Esag. She was the neighbor on the right and people called her Mami Nzelle. She came into the house bringing along some food, which she offered to her new neighbors. They chatted on and on and suddenly she got up to leave, then changed her mind as she pushed the door blind aside to peek out. Taking her position back on the chair, she cautioned Nkongho about the WOMAN from across the street. "You know, she is a prostitute, not so? Number

one ashawo!" Wrinkling her nose in disgust, she added, "She has too many men in her life. I just thought you should know that."
"Thank you," Nkongho said simply.
Mami Nzelle scoffed. "I shouldn't be saying this, but do you know that your left hand neighbor doesn't go to church?" Nkongho gazed at her sheepishly. "Now her children are little devils," Mami Nzelle carried on. Nkongho continued staring at her neighbor not knowing what to say. But Mami Nzelle did not give up. "I really feel sorry for her, you know. Really, I feel sorry for her too much." She sighed. "Such a decent woman," she mumbled. "She is married, you know?"
Nkongho grinned; her mother on the other hand, fidgeted on her seat humming and sighing intermittently. Mami Nzelle stood up one more time and parted the window blind to show Nkongho where bad girls went every night to kill their children. "I don't trust these clinics in the quarters. I don't at all. All they do is kill, my sister." When Nkongho asked her how she knew about it; she said she was usually up past midnight and began describing some of the things she had seen. Nkongho stood up suddenly, went into the room and stayed there. Mami Nzelle was still standing. She stood there in the living room shifting her eyes between the front door and the disenchanted older woman on the cushion chair. She waited and waited. She then took a few steps out the door but poked her head back into the parlor. She fidgeted with the knob, turned it round and round then paused. Finally, she let it go and dragged her whole self back into the room and just stood there with hands akimbo.
"Ah say-eh, Nkongho, fine girl like you, where is your man?" she asked and waited.
Nkongho shouted from the room that she would tell her when he arrived. The woman nodded understandingly. Only then did she leave the house towing her modestly heavy body out of there without a backward glance. At the same time she giggled like an excited schoolgirl all the way to her own verandah where she rested her huge buttocks on the hard plaster of concrete.

Nkongho had not returned to her chair when she heard another knock on her front door. This time it was Mrs. Sama, the neighbor on her left. Like Mami Nzelle, she had brought a bowl of freshly cooked food to welcome her new neighbor. "I saw her leave," she began, "and I thought it was time for me to come too. Did she say anything bad about me?" Without waiting for a reply, she went on. "See, Madam, we are a good family…It's just that when Patron is drunk he beats me and the children. So we cannot go to church on Sundays. "See, we have swollen eyes, and wounds everywhere. Madam, you know, na? One should not let everyone know that one is suffering, na?" She stopped abruptly. Nkongho nodded.

"I see you have one, two, three, four,...How many do you really have sef?" Mrs. Sama asked, shifting her eyes from one angle of the room to another trying to situate the new tenants. "Are they all your sisters and brothers?" Then she realized her mistake. "I didn't mean it that way."

Aunty who had gone into the room as soon as Mami Nzelle stepped out and Nkongho reentered the parlor sighed.

Nkongho sat still and waited. Then Mrs. Sama got up suddenly as she had appeared and headed for the door. "By the way Mr. Esag will want to follow you. Watch out!" she cautioned.

"Why? Isn't his wife enough?" Aunty shouted from the bedroom.

"Whoosh! Is that a woman? They say she never gives him because he always wants her to bathe first...and...and, well...she is like a pig if you know what I mean. But like I say...," she paused. "What's your name again?"

"Epo," Aunty offered quickly poking her face in the parlor.

"Nkongho."

Mrs. Sama was confused. "Okay, Epo-Nkongho, just be careful." On this note, she left.

Nkongho and her mother waited for more knocks as the children yelled at each other in two different bedrooms.

"Aunty, what do you think?"

The older woman shrugged her shoulders. "Let's just wait and see. You know people how they are. Talk, talk all the time. Well, let's just wait and see." She shrugged her shoulders again.

"No, no, not even that. See, what if that man really wants me?"

Aunty stared at her daughter in disbelief.

"Why should he want you? Eh? Epo, do you realize it's time you look after the children you have?"

"I know, but...Well...Aunty, you see,...All right, I will look after them."

"You better! You sit there and even think about that man; don't you think I don't want those kind of people too?"

"I have heard, Aunty. Ah beg, leave it like that"

"I'm glad you have heard." She said this as a matter of fact. "Now push that tray here." Aunty opened the two dishes that had been standing on the table since the two neighbors left. "Ah tell you, Epo, these women have done wonders. The one that doesn't bathe brought stockfish; and the one with the bad children brought egusi pudding!" She smiled. "My daughter, let's eat and forget about their problems."

The children came dashing in the parlor as they heard their grandmother's excited voice.

"Epo, look at your battalion. Food, food, that's all they think about. Glory, bring me a plate let me take our own then you people can fight over the rest."

In no time, the girl, Glory was back with a big enamel bowl. She watched her grandmother dish out some from both bowls.

"Now, take the rest and go, but you people should not scratch these bowls-oh. They are not your mother's, and sometimes, I wonder if she will ever own such lovely bowls...like real women do!"

"Aunty, don't say that. You know very well that I didn't have a nice cupboard to store the few I had. Besides, how many real mothers own good bowls?"

"I can name you lots and lots."

"Try."

"Ah, what's the use? Ah beg, come let's eat before the food gets cold."

They had not finished their food when the door burst open and a woman of about Nkongho's age waltzed into the parlor. She greeted them in their dialect. Without introducing herself, she gently placed two bowls of food, which were neatly carried in a basket covered with embroidered table cloth on the coffee table they were eating at, and washed her right hand in a bowl of water that stood by the table. Nkongho and her mother watched her every movement. They were surprised but not unpleased with her informality. The guest took a bite at the stockfish and began chewing it gracefully.

"This is good, Epo," she complimented. They ate quietly. "Aunty," she addressed the older of the two women she had joined with much ease. "You don't know how glad I am that you people have moved here. Ah tell you, you people will not believe it. These people are so bush! They are so,...How do I put it-eh?"

Aunty cleared her throat as she ate on, waiting to hear what those people were.

"They just don't understand life. When I wear my ready-made dresses, they call me ashawo. When I wear my wax wrapper, I mean real wax, not made in Nigeria or made in Cameroon,...They call me chop money. They are too foolish—these people for this street. Take it from me; I've been living here for God knows how long!" She paused to put more food in her mouth.

"Who are you, my daughter?" Aunty asked in her dialect.

"Oh, me! Ah, Aunty, Sally Ikome. My papa is a man from Soppo; my Sissy is from Muea, but they separated a long time ago. I don't even know how he looks like anymore; but my Sissy,..." she smiled, "comes here all the time."

"Epo, talk to your friend, na. See, my daughter is a nurse—a real one! Epo, tell her yourself, na? Wait, Sally, you have children, not so?"
"Of course, I do Aunty, but let's not talk about them now. Epo, once you settle down we shall do a lot of things together, not so?"
Nkongho nodded.
"Good. Aunty, open that pan and see what I brought. Wait, guess first."
Aunty burst out laughing. "My daughter, Sally, you are too much! I am a Bakweri woman. Of course, I know what it is."
"Just guess."
"Is it kwacoco and banga soup?"
"Yes, Aunty. I put smoked fish; I put kanda; I put meat; I put stockfish; I put everything in there, Aunty. I hope you people like it."
Aunty put a piece in her mouth. Sally waited for the compliment that should follow.
"Sally, you have really done the true Bakweri way. My child just come and elay me." She hugged her affectionately.
"I hear you have a small Mami here, eh Epo? Where is she?"
"Glory."
"Sister."
"Come and greet somebody."
"Okay, Sister." The girl hopped playfully into the parlor.
"So you are Glory, eh? I am Sister Sally. I live over there." She pointed to a house not too far from theirs. "You know, I have a little girl like your small sister, Chinyere, and a boy, Monday's age…no, no, I think she is your age. The boy should be Jacob's age." She paused and gazed at Nkongho stupidly. "How come you gave them those awful names?"
"My daughter, ask her yourself. I've told her several times that they can use the Bakweri names I gave, but would she listen? No! The whole house is packed full with foreign children. I don't know-oh." Aunty shrugged her shoulders resignedly.
"Sally, it is none of your business anyway," Nkongho said calmly. "By the way, what do you call yours? Lyonga, Limunga or what?"
There was silence as everybody waited to hear. Sally shook her head to the contrary. "No, the girl is Elsie, and the boy is David."
"Eh?" Aunty barked.
"Aunty, I'll tell you the story some other day. It is a long story and one night is just not enough."

"I see," Nkongho said thoughtfully. What else could it be? Her friend's face darkened.
"We shall talk about that tomorrow, not so, Aunty?" She stood up and feigned a yawn.
"Epo, see your friend off, na?"
"No, no, it is no problem. My house is not even far sef. Just across the road. You people shouldn't really bother about me. Let me go so you can continue to unpack. I'm sure you people are happy to have left that bush."
Aunty shook her head
"We liked it there," Nkongho said simply.
Sally ignored the comment and bade them goodnight before disappearing into the dark night. They could hear her cracking with laughter as she conversed with somebody not long after. Her shrill voice was so loud they could hear her asking a man when he planned on taking her out again to a chicken parlor. Soon a car drove off and all was quiet out there but for the music that boomed in Sally's small Off License.
"Epo, she is a good girl, not so?"
"Aunty, I don't know. But she must have money to be wearing the things she says she wears."
"What do you think? She has an Off License, na?"
"Yes."
"My daughter, you are pretty too."
"Thank you, Aunty."
Later that night Nkongho cleared the table and went out to draw water from the common well at the back of her rented quarters. She was about to pull the pail from the deep hole when she heard people laughing in the dark. At first, she couldn't make out the voices, but as she stood there quietly for a much longer time, she sensed something vaguely familiar in the laughter and whisperings. She recognized Mami Nzelle's voice and Mrs. Sama's but the third voice she couldn't place. Not knowing why, she tiptoed closer to Mami Nzelle's verandah where the three women sat. They had seen Sally hop into a man's car and were wondering what hotel she was being taken to. One said Sally made single life so appealing she was even tempted to run away; after all, she was barren. Nkongho tried to place this voice as she stood there in the shadows listening on to their conversation. She thought harder and it finally dawned on her who the person was. She sighed and was about to leave when she heard Mami Nzelle narrating a story about her own near barren experience. She said it had taken her as much as two months to get pregnant, even though she had been a virgin when she got married.

Mrs. Sama said hers was worse—six long months! The third woman sighed and made a remark about women like Sally being responsible.
"What do you expect from a pretty woman like that?" Mami Nzelle mocked
"Something more—like she having her own husband."
"Yes, she had one! Well, sort of," Mami Nzelle said. "My sisters, that pretty thing like that is a devil as you see her like that-oh. Her story is a long one."
"Mami Nzelle, she is like Mami Water. So beautiful, it's hard not to notice her. True, if I was a man I would chase and capture her. I don't know why they let her go," the third woman added.
"Sometimes, I wonder why they let her go myself. The other day, I heard my little Paul telling his friends that the woman's breasts were bobby tannap. You know! How can she still have such a firm body when she already had two children? What kind of medicine does she use? Eh, boh? No pimple—skin like a small girl's own!" Mrs. Sama concluded.
"Leave me-oh, my sister," Mami Nzelle began, "One child and my body just sagged like a balloon that has lost its air. So you can imagine what five children did to me. One operation here, long stretch marks there and there; as for my grapefruits, they just turned into two long, over ripe agric pawpaws. Ah, tell you true."
"You people are complaining like that, what about me? Mine are still oranges, but what good are they to me? Patron doesn't touch them, and God doesn't want to give me a baby. Who will suck them? Sometimes, I wonder why he had sent me into this world at all!"
All was still for a moment then Mami Nzelle burst out laughing.
"What is it?" the other two asked eagerly.
"No, it is something I was just thinking about. We are all complaining—just look at our new neighbor. Can you imagine what her own life is like?"
They laughed harder, clapping their hands in wonder.
"They can't fool me, those two! I think it is Nkongho or Epo whatever her real name is that has those children. If you look at her well, you will see a married woman's wear and tear staring back at you. You know how a well used married woman looks like—the kind that looks like she has never enjoyed life. Just born, born from the day she entered a man's house till the day she dies. That's how she looks…Thick fleshy waist, fat flabby stomach that can only be controlled with girdles. I'm sure her own breasts you can actually carry them in your hands and wrap around your neck. Poor thing. And she's definitely unmarried!"
"Ah, ah, Mami Nzelle, how do you know about that?" Mrs. Sama asked excitedly.

"A woman who has a husband mentions him on first contact with new people. Besides, what married woman who is a nurse would want to stay in a plank house?" She sighed. "My dear friends, she's worse off than our beauty queen. She is a suffer woman; I'm telling you people." She said this as a matter of fact. Nkongho stepped out of the dark spot she had been standing all this while and marched over to where these women sat. Without pausing to think, she poured the water she had dragged out of the well on their immobile figures then marched back to get more for herself.

The next morning, dressed in her white nurse's uniform, Nkongho returned all the bowls personally and thanked each woman for being kind. She didn't mention last night's events. Neither did they. At least, she did get to see the interior of their houses too.

CHAPTER 3

Across the street from the Elates was solid evidence of good life, as people flocked around Sally's Off License popularly known as BAR DE NUIT. Sally's little place had beer, sweet drinks and even palm wine. There were some weekends she actually stocked afofo. It was loud at all times. The colorful lights and loud music lured children, fathers, and bachelors; eventually the raucous laughter from the drunken men that visited the place on a regular basis attracted mothers and wives.

Some of these women could be seen every evening fanning red, hot coal in front of BAR DE NUIT as they roasted fish and plantains for the drinkers. The place boomed night after night. Sally had a girl there who attended to the poorer customers—those weh their own no dey, and a boy who ran up town to buy crates of drinks from the depot. If he wasn't stocking up on drinks, he was behind the counter selling drinks to every customer. Well, of course, not to the special ones that Sally would rather serve personally.

No one really knew where Sally had come from. One fine day, she was just there renting one of the best houses on the street. Before people knew it she had opened an Off License. Her life was her business, she kept reminding herself night after night as she put on one fancy dress after another to go out with one admirer after another.

But the simple truth was that Sally had spent a good portion of life right there in Kumba, only no one would believe her if she ever mentioned it. She had been a student at a commercial school in the part of Kumba she no longer visited. A really good student, for she was one of the few from her school who had attempted G.C.E six times and was able to have a pass grade in two ordinary level subjects! She would have continued writing if her mother had not wisely reminded her that all fingers were not equal. But she would not work as a clerk as some of her lucky friends did. Her goal was to break the unspoken rule that commercial college students weren't university material. Perhaps she would have if her mother had just been patient and let her write the G.C.E a few more times. She would never know, for she had abandoned her mother's house and joined some friends elsewhere in town.

Her new home became a big house with lots of rooms. It was clean and spacious and extremely quiet in the day as everybody took a long nap that usually lasted hours. It would be so quiet Sally would wonder what happened to her friends as she lay on her bed reading romantic novels. But at night, it was a different story. One by one, Sally would watch her friends dress up and leave the house only to return in the wee hours, then sleep all day. It was like that every single day she spent with them. Then she got tired of just sitting there and doing nothing. She was neither a student nor a worker. She was just a town girl who did nothing at all—unless one counted reading romantic novels as something. Sally decided to change her life! She agreed to accompany her friends out.

The first night out, she met a man she didn't like. The subsequent nights she met some she admired just a bit. They did not only have money, but spoke good English half the time she was with them. Hearing the story of her life, one offered to buy her current G.C.E questions if she would just…Sally took one look at his potbelly and refused. Her friends were not impressed by her attitude.

"What's your problem?" one of the six friends she was putting up with had enquired.

"Nothing," Sally replied.

"Then accept one of them. See, if you don't like money, why don't you just take it and give us," another coaxed.

"Who says I don't like money? You think it's me who doesn't like to wear good clothes too?"

"Then?" They all barked at her.

"That's not really the problem…" she hesitated, "I just don't know how they do it, if you know what I mean." Her friends exchanged glances.

"Fat lie!" one exclaimed. "Big, fat lie! When we were students you must have tried it once, na? At least, with one of those young teachers."

"No, I swear to God. I'm afraid."

"Afraid, my foot!" the friend who actually had invited her to move in with them muttered. "Well, if you want to take it to your grave, that's your business. Look at me, I've done and done it and each time it's like new. All you have to do is wash it with limestone." She chuckled. "My future husband will never know the difference."

After several futile attempts to reach Sally, her friends stopped bothering her. Sally stopped spoiling their nights out.

She would stroll in the evenings all by herself wondering what to do besides reading Barbara Cartland, and Denise Robbins. Then she stopped by a neighboring bar and just sat on a bench and waited for the night to unfold. It went by slowly as it normally did giving those people who can afford to take a chance a reason to stay up late and enjoy themselves. Sally noticed older men entering with young girls by their sides. She noticed young men in groups of three or four loitering around. Some just stood there conversing; others hummed the tune of the music that was booming from the bar; others just kept pacing from one end of the street to the other idling around. Occasionally, they would walk past the bar. But there was a group of young men that went right in and filled their table with drinks. Sally sat there hoping the night would move along faster. The young men sat in there sipping their beer from glasses and were actually conversing in Standard English. She listened but couldn't understand what they were talking about. She slipped off her seat and headed home. The next day, she was there again, waiting on the same bench. On the third day, one of the young men accosted her. She was confused as to his intentions. He said he was tuning her, all she had to do was say yes or no. Unsure of her feelings, she gave him the usual answer—she needed to think it over. That night she waited up for the others and broke the news to them.

"You say he speaks but English and wears a tie?"

"Yes"

"Sally, don't let him go. Catch him quickly at once. He's in the university."

"Hmm!" Sally was impressed. She beamed all night.

"Can you believe me a university graduate's wife?"

"Boh, he's yours. All you have to do now is give him whatever he wants," her friends advised.

This set the tone to Sally and Simon's relationship. When she finally accepted to be his girlfriend she was ready to do whatever he wanted—and he wanted everything she could offer. It was a union that brought forth two children.

Sally stood by the roadside to wait for Nkongho to step out of the taxi that just pulled up. "Ah, nyango, are these your eyes?"

Nkongho smiled.

"I have spent the whole day talking with Aunty. She's very funny."

Nkongho did not reply.
"Ah say-eh, boh, do you know my house sef? See, it is that one over there—not far from yours even. Can you come there sometime?"
"Sally, I will. Let me just get used to this wuna place first." She sighed. "Too much work; no water, just well, well everyday!" Nkongho replied.
Sally laughed. "You know something? Sometimes you make me laugh. I have my own private pump in my house. Come carry your drinking water from there, na? When I came here too it was well water I used to use, but it gave me a lot of rashes, even though I used dettol. Ah beg, my sister, don't suffer yourself too much."
"Thank you, plenty." Nkongho started moving toward her house. "How is my mother? Is she in a good mood?"
"The best of moods. I just gave her a bottle of Beaufort, but she says next time, I should bring her but Becks." Sally began laughing again.
"That's Aunty, all right."
Nkongho bade Sally bye and entered her house.

It was a strange sight that greeted her. Someone had rearranged the chairs. One stood by the front door; another stood closer to the door leading to her bedroom. The sofa had no cushions at all. The red foam cushions piled on the floor. There were egusi peelings on every piece of furniture, and palm oil had spilled on the white cotton tablecloth she had bought just recently. Nkongho sighed. "Aunty, what is happening in this parlor like this? Who threw oil over here? Whose dirty wrapper is on that chair so-eh?"
"Who else, Epo? Your children! Me and Glory, we try a lot, but when you have children your house cannot be clean."
Nkongho threw her handbag on the chair and went to the kitchen, a small room attached to her house like an architectural afterthought. She opened the pots that stood by the three stone fireplace but found nothing to eat. "Where's my own food-eh, Aunty?" she shouted. "Don't tell me you people starved me again."
"The little ones were hungry, what do you expect?" Aunty screamed back. "There was nothing we could do. Ah beg you, my child, do not be angry. Nobody told us food would cost so much in this your town."
Nkongho stormed out of the kitchen, walked past her mother into their bedroom. While in there, she searched her purse for some money but found only the loose change the taxi driver had given her. She tossed the bag aside, sat on the bed with her nose flaring as her stomach grated from hunger. She got up, paced back and forth and sat down. Got up again, parted the window blinds and peeked outside. She could see Sally standing in front of her house. The woman was munch-

ing something. Nkongho changed into her house clothes; moments later, she was on Sally's doorstep brushing the dust off her slippers before getting into the woman's beautiful parlor. It was the first time she had been there. "Sally, are you there?" she called out, preparing to explain her appearance. "I saw your door open, so I just thought that I should come in."

"Epo, is it you?" Sally called from the bedroom; "Just come in, there's beer in the fridge or are you one of those who drink but worm medicine?" she asked coming out of one room and entering another.

"Yes, boh. Anything sweet."

"Okay, then get it from the Off license; don't forget to tell the boy it's me that sent you." Nkongho got her drink and began sipping it gently. Sally entered the parlor with a comb and thread in her hand. "Have you eaten, Epo?" Not waiting for a response, "There's food in the kitchen, go get some."

Nkongho served herself some pepper soup and took her position back on the chair. Half-way through the meal, she became self conscious and began looking around, really noticing things in the room for the first time.

"Who's that?" she asked as she noticed a picture on the cupboard.

"Oh, my children's father," Sally said indifferently. There was a brief silence.

"He's handsome."

"Yes."

"Where is he?"

"Yaounde."

"Married?"

"Yes," Sally paused then added, "To a doctor, a medical doctor."

Nkongho whistled in awe. "That's the kind of man you befriended?"

"Of course, I wanted a big man. He is something bigger than the Magistrate he was when he took the children."

"The doctor is their mother now, I guess."

Sally frowned and began fidgeting with her hair.

"How do you compare yourself with a woman doctor?" Nkongho asked.

When she got no response she turned around and looked at her friend in the face.

"Sally are you listening?"

"Of course, I'm listening. She's…, well, I don't really know what to say."

"Hmmm! She must be pretty."

"I am prettier."

"She must be young."

"I am younger."

"Then why did he choose her?"

"She's a doctor like you've already remarked."
"I know."
"Then don't ask me again."
"Okay, one more question then no more. How is your life?"
Sally stopped pulling her hair. "What kind of question is that?"
"I don't know, just curious, I guess."
"I am happy."
"Fine then."
"Someone knocked at the door.
"Sister," a voice called.
"Glory, what is it?" Nkongho called back, standing up to put the bowl away.
"Aunty wants you right now."
"Okay." She stood up. "Sally, thanks for the food."
"Thank God."
Nkongho left without noticing the tears that had begun gathering in her friend's eyes.

Chapter 4

The yellow door blind was tied into a knot halfway and the children took ample advantage of this. They dashed in and out the house all day long as they pleased. The yellow door blind never ceased to dangle. Already shredding apart, and with lots of grime on it that stuck on an adult who mistakenly touched it while leaning against the door, there was not much Nkongho could do to salvage the situation. Some friends of Nkongho's children would spend hours punching the blind, wringing it as they reminded themselves proudly that they could make great boxers or wrestlers. The next Muhammed Ali or Bessala. Others made several attempts to swing on it like a see saw. The tattered blind brown with filth guarded the entrance to that house fiercely.

The house stood there at the corner of the junction watching and waiting. Besides its strategic location, it was the only plank house within two blocks of Krammer Street. The landlord had applied a fresh coating of white wash when he heard that someone was interested in it. That was a couple of days before Nkongho had moved there. People said he was a good man, but he had been unable to fix the house because the town council had mentioned something about using part of the building for road construction. And so the house, with its termites and cracked foundation stood there as if it had a future. It wasn't the best, Nkongho told her mother, who had made a big deal about living in a 'calaboat' house. The house had no bathroom, so Nkongho had insisted on the landlord putting up a makeshift one with bamboos, plank wood, and zinc at the back. He had done that; but her children still insisted on bathing in the pit latrine building. They said they preferred bathing behind concrete walls. The latrine flies didn't bother them one bit. And so it was Nkongho and Aunty who used the new bathroom, or at least Aunty did until Sally said she could use her shower and water system toilet whenever she wanted. Aunty accepted and never again stepped foot in the latrine or make shift bathroom.

The guava tree that stood next to their building had begun losing its fresh green leaves too as the children pulled its branches all the time in search of one miserable budding fruit after the other. There was never a day that a child wasn't tugging on one of its branches or stampeding on its narrow trunk. The parents watched without seeing as they went about their business, but every once in a while, a father would gnash his teeth and bellow for the children to stay away from the tree. The children would leave it alone momentarily; however, as soon as the father disappeared they flocked back on it, enjoying its ample generosity and its inability to complain. It was like that, day in, day out, and the only real time it could have a break from restless, tiny fingers was usually when darkness fell or when it rained heavily.

Children clung desperately on its branches hours on end singing and swinging until the tree would gradually wither away. But like a miracle it would be revived after a series of rainstorms. Its green leaves would look so fresh that even the women would not be able to ignore its loveliness. From their distance, they would praise its new fresh look and hope that this time the children would let its hard, green, budding fruits to become soft and yellow, so the adults could taste the fruit too. But it was never so.

The guava tree would sway from side to side under the children and without warning a branch would crack. Only then would the children on that part of the tree quickly jump down and find a string and a heap of concrete to support it from completely collapsing. They would do this not without spreading leaves and soil on Nkongho's verandah and none on Mami Nzelle's.

Nkongho didn't mind at all. She was simply ashamed of her house. She deserved more, she told herself repeatedly. She had taken the trouble to find out what most of the women in their quarter did for a living. The answer was simple! Most of them were just housewives who cooked and cracked egusi all day long when their children and husbands toiled for education and a living. Some actually worked in offices but none could match her rank. She was a trained nurse with her brevete` certificate from Bamenda! If she hadn't given up her job with the company so soon she would belong to a privilege class, and would be hoping to reside in a bigger and better house in the nearest future. But as things were at that moment there was no such hope. She had no illusion about this. She would live her life, taking her fortune and misfortune as it came. Wasn't that what a woman's life was all about? Eh?

But one thing remained clear; she was in Kumba, and here, they not only paid the rents but actually bought water and electricity.

Nkongho walked briskly across the road toward her house immediately she dropped off the taxi from work. Taxis hooted nonstop but she ignored these and wangled her way through the unusually busy traffic until she spotted Aunty, with Enanga, the last born on the verandah waiting. Aunty's lips were glued tight. Her red eyes gazed past Nkongho. She sighed. Nkongho cleared her throat then sighed too. She suspected something wasn't quite right. Things not being quite right was becoming part of her every day reality. If Aunty wasn't in a bad mood, she would be hungry; if she wasn't either of those, it would be the children. Every afternoon or evening as Nkongho returned home from work there was always something the matter. Always! She sighed again and held out her hands to take the child. Aunty sighed too and began walking away as she handed Enanga over.

"Aunty, what is it this time?" Nkongho began.

"You were gone too long and I was beginning to worry."

"Ah, ah you too," she said, heaving a sigh of relief. With the child in her arms, they entered the house.

"No. True, true, I was worried," Aunty said solemnly. "Sometimes, when you go to that your work like that I'm afraid. What if you die—what will I do with all your battalion?" Nkongho put the child down.

"Enanga, go join your sister, Glory or Chinyere." The child trotted away, chuckling and drooling all over the place. "You fear too much, Aunty. Is that all your problem?"

"Oh, no," Aunty replied. They sat down in the parlor. Aunty adjusted her buttocks well on the seat and the cushion burst on the sides. She shifted uneasily and the chair creaked.

"Ah beg, no spoil my chair."

"Ok, my daughter. I hear you," she carried on until she was well seated then she cleared her throat and looked toward her daughter.

"You see, Epo, palm oil is finished; kerosene is finished; meat is finished. Only mbonga and cocoyams in the chop box."

"Then let Glory cook porridge coco, na," Nkongho said exasperatedly as she stood to go into their room. They should all leave her alone, she felt like screaming. Everyday there's something lacking in the house. What did they want her to do? Was she a magician or a married woman who would run to her husband to complain and get some more food money? No!

"Oh, no, no, Epo, you don't listen," Aunty persisted. "I say, no palm oil too. No crayfish and all that other stuff to make it taste."

"Here." Nkongho got some coins from her purse and placed on the table. "Send Glory or Jacob. Anybody. Let them just buy anything they fit with that."
Aunty stared at the three silver coins her daughter had just put down.
"It is only three hundred francs, Epo," she sneered.
"Yes, I know."
"Then?"
"You want me to steal to please you or what, Aunty? That's all; if you people can't buy anything with it then you sleep hungry! Just leave me alone!"
Aunty remained unperturbed. She sat there listening to her daughter rambling on and on. Soon Nkongho began sobbing.
"See me trouble-oh!" Aunty exclaimed, struggling not to lose her temper. "I came to help someone and she has transferred her problems to me. Hmmm! Josephine Elate you have not seen anything yet!" she clapped her hands in bewilderment and began searching the room for something.
"Ah say-eh, who is in that room? Glory?" There was no answer. "Chinyere? Jacob? I know you people are in there." Aunty stood up. "Glory, you come out at once before I lose my temper like your childish mother!"
"Aunty, I'm carrying Enanga."
"Okay, Chinyere, you come."
"I'm cracking egusi."
"Who is there again? Jacob? Simon? James? Monday? Where are those stupid pirates?"
"Don't call my children pirates!" Nkongho screamed from the bedroom she and her mother shared with the female children.
"You shut up there, a woman who can't even feed her own children! Who even told you to have them with poor people? See your friend over there, she looks young like a young girl. You are here looking like it's you who delivered me. If you open your mouth in that room again I'm going to beat the hell out of you. Some foolish thing sef!"
Nkongho burst into fresh tears. The children could hear her crying shamelessly in the room.
"James, you come out here and go to the market at once." Aunty barked. The boy came out sulking. "Aunty, I'm only a small child. What about the others? Monday is older, he is up to nine-years-old. Simon is…"
"Don't you dare call my name in there, you young Biafran!" .
"But is it a lie? I'm just…" he continued to whine.
"James, if you don't shut up your leaky, leaky mouth there, I'll join you and your crying mother and beat the two of you up this instance." Aunty barked again.

"Who even told you that Ibo children are small? Eh? Look at his head like a Bakweri man's own."

Aunty's voice rose with every insult she levied on the child.

"Come take this money this instant and go buy half bottle of palm oil and some small crayfish. Then go meet that your country woman, Ngozi and tell her that I am hungry. Just tell her that me, Josephine Elate, mother of your foolish mother is hungry. Go now!"

She stood there raging as the little boy tore out of the house. "Jacob, Simon and the other Ibibio boy come out here at once." Aunty waited for some minutes, nobody seemed to be showing up. "Okay, no food this evening. That will take care of your stubbornness. Some lazy things! If God had answered my prayers Biafrans should have won that war. At least, they know how to work. What do your people know? Eh? These good for nothings?" The children came rushing into the parlor, laughing their heads out.

"Aunty, what is it you want us to do?" Jacob asked.

She ignored them.

"Eh, Aunty?"

"You, Monday, go draw water from the well; Simon split some firewood; and you Jacob, will cook the porridge."

"But Aunty, what will Glory and Chinyere do? You are cheating." Jacob sulked as he walked away to carry out the instructions. He wasn't too far gone when Aunty began laughing as a thought crossed her mind. "Was your father not a cook? Perhaps you will end up a cook yourself."

"No way, not me." Jacob snorted. He was not angry with his grandmother; just confused at the things she made them do.

Monday and Simon hurried through their chores and took off to play. Jacob waited in the kitchen, a miniature version of their plank house, peeling cocoyams as he anticipated James' return. He heard his grandmother laughing heartily and he knew at once that James had brought something nice. Indeed, he had. Ngozi had sent them some rice, tin tomatoes and sardines. Aunty was beside herself with joy, calling Ngozi the kind of daughter a woman should really have. They had porridge that night, and rice and sardine stew all day long the following day.

Later that night, all the children, including two-year-old Enanga went over to Sally's hot spot to enjoy the glamour that prevailed there. It was something they always looked forward to night after night when they had cleaned up the kitchen and locked up. Aunty and her daughter sat on the verandah, conversing as usual. Not long after Sally joined them with a bowl of kanda stew and a bottle of beer for Aunty. Mami Nzelle sat on her verandah cracking egusi, not bothering with what was going on, on the other side. Her husband came out, stretched his arms, and yawned noisily before mounting his Suzuki and rode off. Mami Nzelle did not budge from where she was, neither did she protest. Her children too had gone to Sally's Off License. As she sat there cracking egusi all by herself Mrs. Sama and the other woman joined her, each carrying a tray of uncracked egusi.

As they sat there cracking egusi she waited for someone to say something new, but none did. They had only old stories to share. Nothing new and exciting. She sighed. Then yawned.

Meanwhile, Nkongho, Aunty and Sally were convulsing with laughter on their own verandah. Mami Nzelle told her friends to be quiet as she craned her neck to catch fragments of their conversation. But each time it would turn out to be nothing juicy—not the kind of stuff she was really interested in. Just boring tales about food and beer. But Nkongho would laugh out so loud that one would think it was something worth listening to. She did this a couple of times and only stopped when she noticed that Mami Nzelle and her friends had moved onto another section of the verandah. Only then did she let down her guard and mentioned something about work and her children. If the others were observing they would have realized that Nkongho and her group were no longer talking, but whispering. Their voices were so low that they found themselves repeating every word. But Mami Nzelle had long given up as she kept sneering at drivers that flashed lights into their faces.

The night had not worn out when suddenly there was a commotion in front of Sally's. It all seemed so innocent to the women, as they thought it was the usual brawl caused by a drunken man then they heard Glory scream at someone. The children in a tight, large circle were cheering and jeering. Others clapped and punched the air excitedly. A kabba here, a hook there and the noise built up.

"Beatam! Kickam for belle. Yes, that's more like it."

The mothers heard them urging someone to beat up another. They could hear Glory screaming that her brother should teach the weakling a lesson.

"Jacob, hold his neck; Yes, box his stomach. Ah say boxam for belle with all your power." She demonstrated punching the air. "Like this, Jacob. Yes, show him that a bastard has plenty power. You call my brother a bastard just because he begged a little bit of your Fanta? You will pay. Jacob, his stomach again. You know what that word means?—a child that doesn't have a father; but my brother has a father. He didn't just fall from a tree, you know? Jacob, throw him on the ground. Show him your Nigerian power. Beat him the way you people beat up those stupid Biafrans. Yes." Glory went on and on. She kept encouraging her brother to beat up Mami Nzelle's son. Jacob kicked and punched harder each time and paused only to stop the blows from his opponent. He scratched and punched relentlessly. The boy would still not cry, even though Jacob was using all his energy; and nobody was willing to separate them. If anything the adults at the off license enjoyed the spectacle, and the bar tender could not abandon his post to intervene. He told James to run home and get his mother. The women were already on their way as the jeers and cheers got louder. They could see Jacob throw one punch and Mami Nzelle's son retaliating with an equally heavy blow. Nkongho grabbed her son, Sally grabbed the other boy and together they pulled them apart.

"What happened here?" Mami Nzelle asked the moment she arrived on the scene. "I say, what happened?" She adjusted her wrapper and headscarf. Her son would not speak but this did not stop her.

"Look here, Jacob, we don't fight in towns-eh. So don't bring that your bush fashion here." She dragged her son away. As soon as they mounted her verandah she began hitting the boy, calling him a weakling. "How can you let a child raised by a mere woman to throw you on the ground like that? Eh?"

The tears that he would not let out during his fight with Jacob began flowing with ease. Mami Nzelle spanked him on his face, back, buttocks, everywhere. He let her beat him. "Let me not catch your foot in that place again, you hear?"

He nodded.

Satisfied, she banged the door in his face and returned to the scene. "Nkongho, we don't fight here. That's the first thing the landlord should have told you when you brought that your battalion here."

"Your stupid son caused it," Glory said boldly as she pushed her mother aside to face this woman.

"I'm talking to your mother and not you. Now get out of my sight! You hear Nkongho, we don't like fight; we are God fearing people. So next time, when your children want to pick a fight tell them to go to Ibo quarters. That's all I have to say." She turned to leave, but Glory would not let her.

"You call us bush people or what? Eh, Mami Nzelle? How are you better than us?"

"Yes, Mami Nzelle, what makes you think you are not bush?" Aunty concurred.

"You people should leave it as it is na? Weh! The fight is over and the woman is going to her house. Just leave it as it is." Mrs. Sama tried to make peace.

"You stay out of it, you this two side cutlass woman. Go to your house before your loving husband beats you again." Nkongho had, had enough of it too. She pushed the women aside and made as though she would charge after Mami Nzelle to settle matters, but Sally restrained her.

"That's our mother! Sister Sally, leave her let her teach that dirty woman a lesson. Leave her!" Glory shouted excitedly.

"No, I won't." Still maintaining a firm grip on Nkongho, she asked everybody to leave her premises. The children dispersed. Aunty hugged Jacob for defending his honor and later gave him fifty francs. To Glory, she gave a bottle of Fanta. She gave Nkongho an expensive George wrapper that had been in her trunk for almost five years. Aunty was in such good-spirits that she began talking about Nkongho's father. How she was just like him. A man who didn't like trouble but always ready to fight if he had to. For the first time since she moved in with her daughter, Aunty brought out pictures of the man who had fathered her children. She showed Nkongho one after the other and that night they cried as she kept saying it wasn't really the man's fault. He had been willing to marry her but Aunty's mother had refused. "You see, Epo, he liked me a lot. He wanted a wife, but my mama said I was too good to be a wife. So he left."

"Just like that?"

"Yes,"

"Aunty, ashia." Nkongho wiped her mother's face. "Weh, ashia."

"Don't worry, Epo. You don't know what would have happened if I had married him. Only God knows."

"Yes."

After the incident at Sally's, neighbours feared Nkongho and her family. They would sit on their verandahs listening to her children insulting one another and sometimes, fighting and crying as they hurt themselves, but no one from the street dare intervened. One moment Glory would refer to Chinyere as a Biafran, the next moment, they would team up against the boys. Soon it would be Chinyere and James versus Jacob and his brothers. Then it would be all of them against Glory and little Enanga. It baffled the people at Krammer Street. Mrs. Sama would spend endless nights on the Elate's verandah listening to the squabbles that usually took place behind closed doors. And when later she narrated every tiny detail to her friends they would sigh and clap their hands in wonder. Mami Nzelle would ask her what she expected from a home where almost every child had his or her own father. When this was said they would concentrate on their egusi, but it was boring just sitting there night after night and not having new gossips. So they diverted their attention to the clinic across the street and the woman who was a perpetual young girl, and left Nkongho and her family alone for some time. They would notice Sally laughing coquetishly and leaning on a man's shoulder, flinging her hand in the air as though she was free of problems—this they didn't like. It would infuriate them so much Mami Nzelle would mum-

ble an insult and spit on the ground. "I don't know why I hate that woman so," she would begin.
"You are jealous," Mrs. Sama would say.
"Me! Are you out of your mind?"
"She looks so happy," the third woman would add.
"Because she is a witch. Have you seen any other happy woman around here?" Mami Nzelle sneered.
"She is pretty," Mrs. Sama remarked.
"And rich."
"So? Can you live in a big empty house like that all by yourself? Ah beg, you people should not bother me, I know she has problems like me too."
The two other women stared at Mami Nzelle.
"Boh, do you have problems too?" the third woman worked up the courage to ask.
"Leave me alone! I don't have any problems. Even if I have what can you do about it? Eh, small girl who got married but yesterday?" She was interrupted by more laughter from the road. "Ah tell you, I really hate this woman. What does she want to show?"

Sally was pretty; she seemed to have more money than their husbands. And as much as they didn't want to think about it, she could easily take their husbands if she really wanted to. Mami Nzelle felt a knot in the pit of her stomach. She bit her lip hard to curb the rage that was slowly building up within her and gradually it went away as Sally and a man took a taxi and drove off. Away from their sight. But then it started building up again as she saw Jacob walking towards his mother's house. He had a bottle of beer in one hand and was smiling contentedly like someone who had just won the lottery. Mami Nzelle could control herself no more. Without thinking, she stood up and screamed, "Son of a harlot!" Once she got this out of her chest, she too began smiling and hurried into her house and slammed the door behind her. The other women left too. Mami Nzelle waited for a few minutes before putting out the light in the parlor. Jacob walked right to the closed door and waited too. It was a tensed moment as he stood out there waiting for the woman to come out and say that rubbish again—if she was the *real* woman she professed to be. When she didn't open the door again, he carefully placed his bottle of beer on the verandah and sprayed concentrated pee all over the wooden door; then he screamed, "Dirty harlot!" and scurried away. The next morning Mami Nzelle scrubbed the wooden door and concrete verandah with Blue Omo detergent and bleach with her bare hands after having watched silently as her husband beat up their son for the stinking mess he had run into when he had returned home late. She heard her son scream for her assistance, but Mami was too ashamed to bail him out. What would she tell her husband—that the headstrong boy from next door had done it? And why?

CHAPTER 5

After that incident everyone on Krammer Street learned his or her lesson. Mami Nzelle in particular knew better than to mess with her neighbors. That boy, Jacob dey-ho, she reminded herself quietly. She smiled and could not curb the joyful feeling that was bursting inside her. That boy was truly something! Who could have really thought that he would urinate on their door? She chuckled as she visualized Mr. Esag's hand on the wet door knob. And that Nkongho sef! Mami Nzelle still didn't know what to make of the woman.

Like a good neighbor, she continued to mind their business anyway, and weeks dragged into months. All was well with the Elates until Mami Nzelle heard a commotion next door. It was Chinyere this time. The tough girl crying? Wonders would never end. At first she ignored them, but when the moaning continued she had to intervene.

"Aunty-oh, Aunty-oh!" Chinyere carried on.

Shut up, your dirty mouth there, Chinyere. Bring manyanga at once, Jacob. Spoon, bandage. Enanga, ah beg you don't die," Glory pleaded with her mother's last child. She lifted the girl up from the bed and rushed her into the parlor where there was more space. The child was burning with fever. "Ah beg you, no die. Simon, what is it? Jacob, the spoon, you fool! James, a basin of water. You people should hurry up. Simon-oh! Time."

"I can't read the clock, Sister."

"Where's Aunty for goodness sake? How can she go and plait her hair at a time like this?" She ranted. "Jacob, come-oh, come-oh. Ah don die-oh."

Enanga's legs kicked forward uncontrollably; her arms likewise as she foamed non-stop in the mouth. Her forehead burned even more.

"Use the manyanga. Pour it all over her. Quick, Sister, pour it on Enanga before she dies," Chinyere yelled.

Glory obeyed. She poured this stinking kernel oil all over Enanga's convulsing body; she put some into the toddler's nostrils, but the child continued to wriggle in her sister's arms.

"Give me the spoon." Enanga's hand punched her in the stomach. She adjusted the little girl on her lap. "Okay, give me the spoon now." Jacob did.

"Wrap the bandage around the spoon first, na. Weh!"

Glory forced Enanga's mouth open and shoved the bandaged spoon between her teeth.

She smiled. "Now, the teeth will not grind again."

Nkongho's children were confused as they handled their sick sister. Their mother had not yet returned from work and somehow Sister Sally too was not around. Amidst tears and screams, Glory struggled to keep the sick child alive. The house was in a state of chaos, as her brothers ran back and forth to fetch one item after the other. Without waiting to be told what to do, Chinyere ran across the street to see if Sister Sally had returned from wherever she had gone. But before the woman could arrive Mami Nzelle had already taken over.

"Pit latrine quick, my child," she ordered.

"All right, Mami Nzelle."

"Ah say, quick."

Glory tried to get up from the chair but sank back into the cushion.

"Give me the child," Mami Nzelle ordered, extending her arms to take Enanga. They ran to the pit latrine.

"Mami, let me do it. Let me help you."

"No time. The child is dying. Hold the door, Glory. Sally, you prepare more manyanga." Mami Nzelle brought the child's head close to the latrine that stunk like hell. Fat-bellied flies buzzed their way out at this sudden intrusion. This didn't deter her. She pushed the child's head further down into the hole. The hot stench hit Enanga's nose and she began coughing and crying.

"Alleluiah!" they all chanted.

"Now, Sally, you take her. Wash the child and pour some more manyanga on her body. No more into her nose." She paused before turning to face Glory. "You are truly a small mami, my child."

Glory beamed and wiped off the last trace of tears from her swollen eyes. Together with her siblings she tailed Sister Sally back to the house to continue Enanga' s treatment.

By the time Aunty and Nkongho arrived home all was fine. Enanga was sleeping, but Glory would not place her on the bed for fear she would die in her sleep. She held the little child gently in the curve of her arm and sat on the chair with a plateful of egusi she was cracking for tomorrow's supper. The boys were in the kitchen preparing the evening meal and Chinyere was outside washing clothes. Nobody said a word to the two grown-ups who had just walked in. Everything seemed to be in order just the way Aunty and Sister Nkongho had left it that morning. The wrapper Aunty had left on her favorite chair, the only chair without loose spring, lay there untouched. Chinyere's tray of egusi sat on the dining table, which they used primarily for studying and cutting fabric. All four foam cushioned chairs with their red covers stood on their usual spots. No trace of any having been moved at all. And the children, well, they went about their business as usual. So Aunty and her daughter could never suspect that anything had gone wrong in their absence.

But after supper Mami Nzelle and Sally paid a follow up visit to see how Enanga was faring.

"Aunty," Sally began, "you have a small mami in your house. This your Glory showed wonders today"

"Ah tell you, Nkongho!" Mami Nzelle concurred. "You know Enanga had convulsion today?"

"What?" Aunty and Nkongho exclaimed at the same time, jumping to their feet to check on the child. Glory was right beside her on the bed, monitoring her heart beat every five minutes or so. She just stared at them speechless. Nkongho burst into tears. With a motion of the hand she bade them to leave the room. Glory and Aunty obeyed. They left her there to be with her youngest child all by herself, something she could not remember doing for a very long time.

"Convulsion, where did that one come from too-eh?" she asked no one in particular. Then moved closer to feel Enanga's body. It felt warm against the back of her palm. Enanga's forehead was wet with tiny balls of sweat. The child smelt of manyanga. On a stool by the side of the bed where Glory had sat stood an empty cup and stubs of tablets Glory had administered to the girl. Sister Nkongho burst into fresh tears. Her last-born could have died in her absence. Her whimpering grew louder and Enanga stirred on the bed. Nkongho quickly dried her eyes and continued to watch her until the child seemed to be deep in her sleep again.

When she joined the others later in the parlor she looked disheveled. Her puffy eyes looked so funny Glory couldn't help but laugh.

"Glory, weh, mami. Thank you plenty."

"Your children showed wonders today. Even your male children," Mami Nzelle congratulated her. "They are women, ah tell you, those boys of yours."
"Thank you, Mami Nzelle."
Mami Nzelle shook her head in disbelief and ignored Nkongho. She was still too stunned from the day's event. "Ah tell you, those boys, hmm! You know how it goes, a man who is not only a man. They are male women!"
"They knew what to do. By the time Chinyere came for me they had already begun taking care of the situation," Sally added.
Nkongho and her mother kept clapping their hands in disbelief as they listened. Each time Sally or Mami Nzelle would say more and the conversation dragged on and on. It was the first time all three of them in that neighborhood were on the same side. The first time they were really not gossiping about each other. They looked so happy sitting there and chatting about Nkongho's children's feat—so happy that they completely forgot that one was a married woman, the other a free woman and the third a mother of children who had no fathers. The conversation carried on until Mami Nzelle's husband began shouting for her. It was a reality Mami would have loved to postpone but how could she with her husband bellowing out there in the dark for all to know that he owned her. She sighed, "I am sure he is hungry. He wants me to heat up his food." As she got up to leave without answering her husband Sally got up too,
"Weh! Sally, weh! Mami Nzelle, thank wuna plenty. It was kind of you people to have helped," Nkongho said, casting her grateful eyes but at the door where Mami Nzelle stood contemplating whether she should run or walk back home.
"Thank God," Mami grunted and disappeared."
"Tomorrow, na?" Sally said simply. "I will bring some pap for Enanga in the morning."
"Okay, my child. Thanks for wuna good work," Aunty replied gratefully, and she really meant it from the bottom of her heart.

Later that night Mami Nzelle related the entire story to her friends. They too were as shocked and impressed as she had been when she had seen Efeti trying to revive the sick child. As if planned the three women sitting on the verandah clapped their hands simultaneously in wonder finding the story incredulous. And for a moment they remained silent as each thought about her life. Mami Nzelle asked herself several times in her mind if any of her children could actually take control of such emergencies. No, she finally said out loud enough for her friends to hear.
"Boh, these children who do not have fathers can really be something-oh."

"I know, na. Hard life gives one strength, don't you know?" Mrs. Sama replied. "Too much suffer ah, ah, my sister. Why would they not be tough?"

They retreated into their silent world again. All that could be heard disturbing the peace of the night besides the loud music booming from Sally's Bar de Nuit was the sound of the egusi they were cracking. Even at Nkongho's all seemed too quiet. One by one people disappeared from the street as the night wore off and was gradually becoming tomorrow. But the three women remained seated on Mami Nzelle's verandah.

"That Glory-eh, I just don't know what kind of child she is," Mami Nzelle broke the silence.

"She is a woman child, what do you expect, eh Mami Nzelle?" Mrs. Sama paused then continued, "You know, they are the best kind of children to have. I'm telling you, Mami."

The others nodded in agreement. But after a moment's reflection Mami Nzelle shook her head in disagreement. "Not really-eh," she started. "Nkongho's boys are like women children too. See that her Jacob sef, he is..."

"Boh, how can you even say a thing like that? Those boys are barbarians. They fight like the tigers they are," Mrs. Sama interrupted.

"No, that wasn't what I meant. I didn't say they were weak; no, they are not that kind of women boys. They are strong like man pickin but have common sense like woman pickin."

"Oh, I see." Mrs. Sama nodded understandingly. "My Patricia is like a man. Not strong, not that kind of a man if you know what I mean. She cannot take care of herself one bit! Cry, cry all the time. If she is hungry, she wants me to go to the kitchen and look for food for her; if she is tired, she doesn't want anybody to disturb her. If she has something good, she hides it and eats alone. That's my Patricia, a typical man child!" Mrs. Sama spat on the ground in disgust. They all burst out laughing.

"I wonder who will marry that kind of woman." The third woman who had been unusually quiet chipped in.

"My sister, isn't that the problem? I think about it all the time myself."

"My own girls are not as bad, but I think if I am not there they can die. I swear to God," Mami Nzelle said.

The other woman sighed dejectedly. "What of me who doesn't even have half a child na? You people just sit there and talk about your weak children, how about me?" She began to cry. As though it was a sign of bad luck, Mr. Esag bellowed and Mami Nzelle packed her tray of egusi and bade her friends good night. And so ended that particular evening.

Two weeks later Enanga was up on her tiny feet again trailing after her older siblings. Aunty never left home again for a lengthy period of time without her. She would carry her on her back and walk slowly to her destination and back at home with the child safely in her care. Or she would stroll with her until they arrived at their destination. Nkongho felt more comfortable with this new arrangement. And went on with her role as the breadwinner of the family. Month after month she would sit in their bedroom and calculate how much she owed Sally; also how much she owed Ngozi and some other kind traders in the market. The bills were mounting and her children were growing. However, hard as she tried she was unable to make ends meet. And before long she began stealing and selling drugs from the government clinic where she worked like she had seen some of her colleagues doing. With Ngozi's help she was able to settle the more aggressive creditors and life continued.

But her peace didn't last long, for the head nurse caught her in the act. He threatened to report her to the authorities if she didn't share the money with him. She did but he still wouldn't let her alone. He would assign her to some of the most difficult patients. Those who were constantly sick but never accepted medication. All they did was call the nurse and complain about their illness. Some man di always witch them and they knew who this relative was. That poor one who cannot feed the battalion in his house! Or that rich one who has specialized in selling people for nyongo!

The head nurse enjoyed watching Nkongho run back and forth the female ward and her tiny office like a headless chicken. He also put her on two to nine shifts for two months, instead of her usual nine-to-two shift. And then off to night duty. This continued like this for several months. Then one day he said he liked her—just like that. She was a very hardworking woman, and he would like to make her his second wife. This was shocking news to Nkongho. She ignored him from then on making sure she took a different path to the wards or to her office. Was he crazy? What did he see in her? Why would a man like him leave all the young, single attractive nurses and fall for her? Something was really wrong somewhere. And so she thwarted his advances for a couple of weeks. But the man would not leave her alone.

He kept slapping her fat behind each time Nkongho accidentally ran into him, or whenever the opportunity presented itself. He would corner her in the crowded corridor and whisper something in her ears. Nkongho would beam all the way to her office or to the ward not minding the patients anymore. Her heart thumped and her hands shook a bit. This was too much! As Nkongho glowed and began looking radiant every day the head nurse slapped her butt harder and watched her skip on the corridor wriggling her makandi vigorously. Eventually, she succumbed and did not hesitate to let him use her body as he wanted. Night duties became her regular shift for as long as she wanted. It was no longer bad as before. It was now a time for enjoyment and she and her boss maximized those moments.

She began spending more time painting her face and lips, and would squeeze into tight girdles and corset bras to control her flabby body. And she did not think twice now to spend money on her hair. The debts could wait a bit longer. Her hair had to be perfect, not the amateurish hairdo she had put up with for so long from her daughters. Nkongho also began to look prosperous. To Aunty this was a sign of hope. Her daughter was not the stupid woman she had truly believed she was. She was shining with cheap big gold plated earrings that dangled all day on her ears. Her feet were now graced with well-polished okrika leather high heel. Nkongho swung her hips walking in style like a woman who knew how to do it better. Aunty just marveled. Hmm! The future could be bright after all.

It did not take long for the neighbors to notice too. Soon it was the talk of Krammer Street as Aunty boasted in front of people at Sally's off license that her daughter was still capable of attracting a man. Nkongho was not off the road as everybody had believed, Aunty announced wherever she could find an audience. Even Sally was shocked at this outburst and when she gave her friend a second look she saw nothing but a mother. A woman with flabby everything and cheap clothing. This was all she could see, not someone's wife or mistress.

Aunty's boasting came to an end when the man visited them one day and said he preferred little Glory instead. Aunty gave him one look and told him he was a stupid beef. He left and never returned and Nkongho went back on a nine to two shift.

It wasn't long after that that Mola Peter who had disappeared forever like the others paid them a visit, bringing along a sack of rice and a carton of tin tomatoes. Nkongho was not in as usual, but he waited all the same. He waited and waited even when Aunty was tired of keeping him company and all the children had gone out to play. He sat there and waited. Aunty wanted to go over to Sally's for some beer but he would not let her move an inch. She became irritated and stopped conversing with him, but he rambled on and on about his miserable life with a woman who did not have a First School Leaving Certificate. How she had broken all his breakable plates; how she did not even know how to waltz the way Nkongho did; how until the day she entered his house she did not have the slightest idea of what a sandwich was. She was too local, he concluded. His former boss, who had returned to Liverpool two years before he had married, would have really been disappointed with him. Aunty merely nodded and waited for him to shut up. At last, he got up and bade her good bye. She didn't answer.

As he was leaving she walked over to Sally's and laid on the couch to wait for her beer and pepper soup. But when Nkongho came later she would not tell her about the visit. Well, until Sally hinted her friend.

"Okay, so you had a visitor today," Aunty said reluctantly.

"Who was it?" Nkongho asked taking a bowl to get her own pepper soup.

"One of your lost men," Aunty said, then hesitated before adding grudgingly, "Enanga's father."

Nkongho's eyes brightened up.

"What was my black, white man doing here-eh?"

"How should I know?"

"He came to see you, Epo," Sally volunteered. "And he brought some food too."

"Hmm!" Nkongho was impressed. "Wonders shall never end. He actually remembered that children eat also."

"Sister, he is a drunkard," Glory remarked.

"What's your business there?" Aunty snapped, "Anyway, he says he will send us some meat for Xmas." Aunty sipped her beer. "One other thing."

"Yes."

"He wanted to find out if Glory had written the Common Entrance."

"And what did you tell him?"

"The simple truth; it is none of his business."

"Yes, Aunty, that's really true," Glory concurred.

"What?"

"Sister, it's none of his business. Aunty is right." She grabbed her grandmother's Beaufort and gulped down a frightening amount of beer. The women exchanged glances and sighed.

"Glory, now I see why you like beer so much," Jacob who had just walked in reproached.

"And where did you come from. Sally's house is for women only."

"Hush, Glory. Come on in Jacob. My house is your house."

"Any way, I don't drink beer."

"Yes, you do. Anyway, Aunty, I came to tell you that the others are hungry."

"Tell your mother."

Nkongho finished her pepper soup and rinsed the bowl in the sink. "Okay, let's go home and figure out what we should make. Glory, oya. Sally, we go see."

They all transferred their bickering to the other house. Glory finished the rest of Aunty's beer as they walked into their parlor.
"Aunty, you see what I mean?"
"Jacob, leave me alone. I've told you several times that I don't drink beer."
"Glory, no lie, you di drink," the others who had been waiting in there concurred.
"Stay out of this you war starter." She barked at James.
"Don't call my brother names, Sister Glory. Is it not true that your father is a drunkard?" With lightning speed Glory slapped her.
"When people speak bad about me, you too, my own sister speak? Eh, Chinyere?"
She slapped her again.
"Shut up, Glory. If you touch my daughter again I will beat you like pounded foofoo," Nkongho yelled pulling Chinyere away.
"So what did he want again, Aunty?" She carried on from where they had left off.
"Basically, nothing. I know that type." Aunty gave Nkongho a warning look.
"Mola Peter is just lurking around waiting for that time when Glory will be a rich man then he will come in and announce to the world that he had fathered her after all. Be careful Nkongho."
"Don't be too hard on him, Aunty."
"I'm telling you; they are all the same. But we are not foolish, my child. Our children remain with us whether they are people or not. When I die you make sure they remain with you." At that moment Sally entered the parlor again swinging her house keys around her tiny finger. Enanga ran to embrace her as the older children ran to the Off License to listen to music and drink the beer remains in abandoned bottles.
"So what's the big problem now, Aunty?
"My daughter, Sally, I was just telling your sister here that a woman should never let a man take her children away from her. Don't you agree?"
Sally and Nkongho exchanged glances and burst out laughing.
"Why are you two laughing? Eh?" Aunty sat up. "You two think I'm foolish, not so? Some day you will see what I am saying." She got up to leave. "You are a foolish girl, you this Sally. I knew there would be traitors like you; only I never realized I would be eating in one 's house. I pity the woman who gave birth to you. Foolish girl that dashed her children to a man, so she can be free to sample more men. I spit on you."
With that Aunty banged the door and walked somewhere, yelling insults at any driver who made the error of flashing lights in her face. She was going to aim

stones at a few but Glory noticed in time and ran over to pull her away from the road.
"Glory," she began, panting as she dusted her hands on her Cicam wrapper. "My Efeti, your mother doesn't know anything at all about life. We work hard to raise children then when they are big men or thick madams those people show up. When they are thieves no one shows up. Is that fair? Eh, my child?"
"No, Aunty."
"Good. I want you to remember that all your life whether I am here or not."
Glory nodded and led the older woman back into the house.

When Mola Peter arrived the following day the children and grandmother left him and his one time girl friend. With the rest of the family gone the room seemed sort of big as these two former whatever selected adjacent seats in the parlor Nkongho had taken the trouble to tidy up a bit for this meeting. Mola noticed and nodded in approval.
He crossed and uncrossed his legs several times and each attempt sank him further into the cushioned chair whose springs seemed to have lost their elasticity. His buttocks squeezed out of the side holes the worn out springs had created. He could actually feel the bottom of his seat touching the floor. Mola adjusted his entire body on the chair and sat forward, then he began tapping the tip of his well-polished black leather shoes. He tapped the shoes nervously on the plain concrete floor. The noise irritated Nkongho. She sighed and waited. It was a strange experience for both of them as they sat there staring each other in the eyes and not really knowing what to say. He belched several times and each time the smell of stale beer would fill the room. Nkongho looked away.
"I brought you people something yesterday," he ventured suddenly.
"We saw it."
He cleared his throat and belched again. "I will be sending you some meat this Xmas."
"I see."
He cleared his throat and beamed.
"Is it rotten meat?" she added as an afterthought.
"No, no, no," he protested. "It is our njangi meat. We are killing a whole cow this time."
"Oh. Then we shall be expecting it."
He cleared his throat again and pretended to scratch his ankle. "I see Glory already has tangerines." He chuckled after saying this and looked away. "Time really flies."
"Yes, time really flies."

"A small girl like that already having tangerines. Time flies-oh!"
"Do you want to suck her tangerines too?" Nkongho asked this question out of the blue.
"What?" Mola barked. The pupils in his eyes dilated as he knitted his eyebrows in disbelief.
"I said do you…"
"I heard you before, you woman with no shame." He was trembling in his seat and tried to stand up at first with no luck. Finally, with full force he pulled himself off the chair.. "Look here," he warned her, pointing his index finger in her direction and pacing back and forth, "God will punish you for that statement, you hear? You must really be a bad woman. Now, I see why God protected me from you." He picked up his hat and fidgeted with his trousers that couldn't stay put around his fleshy waist. Nkongho watched him struggle. He unfastened the belt and moved the buckle one hole forward to tighten it. It worked. He looked short with the mass of flesh he had accumulated over the years. One thing remained though; he still carried his little radio everywhere with him.
"I am leaving," he grunted. "I will still send you the meat and if possible a crate of sweet drinks, but you are a bad woman, you hear? A very bad woman—not good for any kind of man at all!" He paused. "Bye, bye na and take care of Enanga and Glory." Mola stumbled out of there without a backward glance. BBC was announcing something on the radio. He shut off the noisy box on his way out, quickening his steps. Mami Nzelle saw him walk like a woman who had been kicked out of her matrimonial home for bad behavior. She rallied her friends and immediately they tried to figure out what had transpired in there. They spent the rest of the evening trying to figure out which one of Nkongho's children had that man for a father.

Meanwhile Nkongho could taste the sweetness in her mouth as she relished how nature had finally treated Mola, the tall slim man who had dumped her for a village virgin. She was so content that she would have told anybody, including the three women on Mami Nzelle's verandah whatever they needed to know about the man with the old radio set permanently on one station—BBC. The man with the bush wife. All they had to do was ask her and she would have gladly told them that it was Enanga and Glory's father despite the fact that they both looked so much like her. It was the man she would have loved to keep for always, and served wholeheartedly. Only like the man said, God did not approve of her. She sighed. "Let him take his bad luck and go away." And like that she forgot about him and laughed hysterically not knowing why. "Oh Nkongho, your own dey-oh!" She laughed hard and soon tears gathered in her eyes and before she knew it they were flowing down her cheeks. She did not know whether they were tears of joy or pain. The tears just flowed. And she let them flow generously soaking her.

CHAPTER 6

That Christmas came and passed and everybody was happy with the food and drink Mola Peter had sent. But the Christmas after that he did not send anything. He did not write, neither did they try to contact him. Soon nobody mentioned his name in the house. Like the other fathers whom they had not talked about for years, and neither had they heard from, he was forgotten in no time! And life went on as usual. And the years flew by.

Glory was growing bigger. If her father had visited them again he would have remarked that instead of tangerines she now had oversized grapefruits that bounced on her broad chest like huge soccer balls. Her fat buttocks were constantly undulating underneath the short gray skirt that was her college uniform. She was as tall as her mother now at five feet, five inches and looked like the chubby woman whose curved short legs stood firmly on the ground at all times; only her flesh wasn't flabby—not yet. She had developed a very thick waistline that was much broader than most of the belts Sister Sally had handed down to her. There was no trace of Mola Peter on Glory's body, so Aunty kept bragging. It just showed how weak of a man he was. A man who would father a child that looked completely like the woman who had carried her in the womb for so many months. Aunty was heard saying this all the time. Glory looked somewhat like her mother and somewhat like Aunty, her granny. She was a cheerful child that had "bad mouth" like the grandmother, and never hesitated to use it whenever necessary. She was every bit like these older women from her head to her toe. It pleased Nkongho and Aunty so much! She was every inch theirs, unlike Chinyere who was lanky and too tall for a girl. Those kinds of girls who looked like boys.

Anyway the older women were proud of both girls. They were proud of Glory, for completely looking like them and of Chinyere, for liking book too much. What Glory had was common sense, Aunty reminded her daughter each time the girl's report card was crowded with "below average" comments written in red bold letters. Was she too not in secondary school, Aunty would ask at nobody in particular.

But Sally's daughter thought Glory was a prostitute who paraded as a student in an unaccredited secondary school that admitted anybody who had money to pay for that kind of education. From the day she and her brother drove into town they would have nothing to do with her. Glory didn't pick their height either. Dressed in one of Sister Sally's hand-me-downs, she would bounce into the older woman's kitchen and take whatever she liked and leave without as much as wishing Elsie good morning. This was too much for Elsie and one day she forbade her from coming to her mother's house again. That did it. Glory picked her up from the comfortable couch she was sitting and running her mouth, and shook her a couple of times before dropping her down like a log. Then she told her to go back to their civilized world if she couldn't stand the way they were living their lives. That evening Sally found her daughter crying on the couch and saying she wanted to go back home where she really belonged. Without finding out why, Sally ran all the way across the street and gave Glory a piece of her mind. Elsie was her daughter she reminded them; Nkongho and her battalion should respect that. They should treat her daughter with the utmost care because she was not like them who have endured suffering all their lives. She was a girl who was accustomed to certain ways. The civilized way of living. A child who wasn't used to strange people walking into their house and taking things without asking. Those kind of people who feel too free in other people's houses! Elsie was that kind of child whose father didn't let quartier children to even lean on their fence. Sally rambled on and on about her delicate daughter who liked privacy. When Glory attempted to explain her own side of the story Sister Sally would not listen. So they let her lecture them about Elsie's right to kick out whomever she wanted from her house. After putting them in their place she returned home and apologized on Glory's behalf. But Elsie still left anyway, refusing to take the money Sally had carefully set aside for her. She said her father had given her enough for the trip. Much to Sally's chagrin Elsie would not take the dresses she had bought as well. She said her Mommy always did her shopping and she would be annoyed if she saw strange dresses in her wardrobe. There was nothing else Sally could do than to watch her only daughter without much ado pack the Prince suitcase she had brought and walk out of her home for her Mommy and real father's house.

The very next day Sally cooked food and went over to make peace with Glory. All was settled and life went on as usual.

But as fate would have it several months later Glory began spitting. Nkongho knew at once what had happened, even though her daughter kept saying all was fine. She would watch Glory take one step and pause to spit, then gnaw on Calabar chalk to fix her mouth. The smell of cooked food would upset her stomach so badly she would vomit nonstop for several minutes. But Glory continued to swear to God that all was fine. Perhaps she had a stomach virus or an ulcer, she would interject as she gathered more spit in her mouth and spat out. At nights she slept with an empty tomato can by her bed and would spend the entire night disturbing her sisters as she kept getting in and out of bed to spit. And one night Chinyere heard her whimpering and immediately she woke up her mother and grandmother. One look at Glory's pitiful face said it all. Aunty sighed in disgust and told her to get out of their sight. Glory attempted to get up but could not as her wrapper got entangled with one loose spring of their family bed. That instant Aunty walked over and gave her one spank across her spitting mouth.

"One more thing," she hissed, "if you stop spitting all of a sudden I will butcher your head. You hear? Harlot!"

Glory burst into more tears. That didn't evoke any sympathy from Aunty who went back to her bed to complete her interrupted sleep. She couldn't, for Nkongho too had begun sobbing.

"You too stop your stupid mouth let someone sleep," she barked from under the old quilt she used as a cover. Nkongho wiped her eyes and blew her nose. Glory continued to cry.

"And you too over there, Glory," Aunty shouted from her side of the room. Then she wiped off tears that had begun gathering in her eyes.

"What a waste of fine food! If you had only been patient, you this Glory, you would have been fine food for a rich man who would have given you a home like the one Elsie lives in. You went and dashed it to a small boy. Bush thing!"

"Aunty, don't say things like that. She is just a child," Nkongho pleaded.

"Bad luck children!"

The boys heard all the noise and one by one they began entering the women's room; before long they were all sprawled on the floor as they pondered the fate of their mother's first born. Like their grandmother, they too were disappointed with Glory and didn't hesitate to tell her so. Because they could no longer go to sleep they had an emergency family meeting then and there and decided that they would not let the neighbors know what had befallen the family. From then on they spoke but in their dialect as they tried desperately to hide Glory's shameful condition from the rest of the world.

This charade did not escape Mami Nzelle. The sharp-eyed woman she was, with an ear for gossip, she could sense something was amiss. She hung around her neighbor's night and day listening on to their conversation and would sometimes sit on their verandah all by herself watching. The Elates pretended not to notice her and went about their business with Glory struggling to be her normal self. Mami Nzelle discussed the situation with her other friends who decided they should all keep watch. After a week of hovering around they began suspecting the girls and changed strategy. Now Mami Nzelle had to watch only Chinyere and Glory closely. She would spend long hours on the verandah looking at them, but each time she would be forced to dismiss the thought from her head. But she just had this hunch that one of them must be pregnant.

"No, no," Mrs. Sama protested, "it must be Nkongho herself. She may be having an old age baby." The other woman listened attentively then sighed as a thought crossed her mind.

"Perhaps one of them is sleeping with one of our husbands," she dared to suggest.

"Not mine-oh!" Mrs. Sama quickly denied, casting a strange look at Mami Nzelle.

"Not mine also, and don't look at me like that. My husband is not the only woman wrapper in this quarter."

"Perhaps it's even my husband," the other woman said resignedly. They all shrugged their shoulders and continued to listen carefully as noises came from the big termite infested house whose white wash coating had long faded away. A bed creaked and the aluminum zinc rattled as someone aimed stones through a hole in the ceiling to the leaky roof. Soon there would be shouts of rat-eh, rat-eh as rushing feet stamped on the rough concrete floor. Then there would be loud laughter and jeering. Just their normal daily activities. Nothing to suggest what Mami Nzelle suspected. But she wouldn't give up trying to figure out what it was the Elates were hiding. Feverishly, she hung around their verandah, back windows and sometimes she would be caught peeking as Nkongho and her daughters took their regular morning baths. Unable to contain it anymore, Chinyere went and reported her to Mr. Esag and he gave his wife the beating of her life. This still didn't stop Mami Nzelle from peeking through holes on the bathroom walls. Glory threw a bucket of soapy water on her; Nkongho hit her with a stick; Aunty levied insults at her. Her husband beat her up a couple more times but she kept lurking around like a bad spirit. Finally, the Elates decided to act fast before it got too late. She was an evil woman they concluded as they made a new plan to save their family's name from more damage.

Aunty advised Glory to drop out of school at once before it became evident that she was with child, instead of repeatedly asking for permission to stay at home to look after her ailing grandmother, an excuse that was becoming a cliché in the principal's ears. It was only then that they forced her to reveal the name of the father of the unborn child. She sort of did. With Sally's help they located him easily. He was one of her clients, a bank manager. The four women went to his office one morning and presented him with a bill for damages caused or else…! The man said he was not the only one.

"How many men can impregnate a woman, eh, you this man?" Sally demanded. She was now quite furious with this man, thinking of the times she herself had spent with him in several four star hotels.

"Get out of my office, crazy women," he thundered, "or else I will call the police."

"Go ahead, call them and I will call child welfare. See something." Glory brought out a notebook. "Each time I met you I wrote it down in this my book. So it's you; don't deny it!"

"Yes, don't deny it," Aunty concurred.

"Okay, it's just three times that I saw you, na? How can I make you pregnant when it takes more than that to get my wife in the family way?"

Nkongho pulled a chair and sat down. She was beginning to get angry.

"See, Patron," she began, "I was foolish at first, but no more. You don't do as we say, my Glory will move into your house this very afternoon. You sleep with my fifteen-year-old, you pay the price."

"How can a girl who does it the way she does be only fifteen?" The man scoffed. You people are really strange. Look at her chest, they are even bigger than yours—all six put together. Big, ripe agric grapefruits."

"Now, we really know what you have been doing to this child. For your information this is her birth certificate." Nkongho extracted a folded piece of paper from her handbag. The man slumped on his seat and sighed. "Weh! What have I got myself into this time-eh?"

"Now you believe us, eh?"

He sat up. "Okay, okay. What is it you people want from me, na?"

The three older women exchanged glances.

"How much?" the man repeated.

"500,000frs." All four of them replied this time.

He opened the top drawer of his desk and gave them cash. The 10,000 francs bills were crisp and new. He watched Sally count them and nodded at the others. "Okay. You people have the cash. Just leave my office and make ah not hear my name again as the father of that child."
The women ignored him and walked out of the air-conditioned office. As soon as they stepped into the street Aunty patted her granddaughter on the back. "Is this not how a woman should behave, eh, Epo? Make them pay. See me some bush man who thinks that because a child looks big she is ready."
"Aunty, leave me-oh," Nkongho interjected. "How can someone pluck a fruit that is green from a tree and eat just because it looks big-eh? Eh, my sister, Sally?"
"Ah tell you, Epo, it is more than me-oh!" She cast one look at Glory's swollen bosom and plump, smooth body. The girl's grapefruits were bouncing up and down like balls. As they bounced, her buttocks swayed from side to side, each time a corner of her short, pleated skirt would move up a bit revealing a portion of her beefy bare thighs. In the bright sunny day it looked fairer than the other parts of her body. It had a soft delicate look like that of a child who grew up in a senior service home. Only her flat, chapped feet contradicted that too well as she walked on high heels that seemed to be going backwards whenever she pulled herself forward. Then her broad back would swell, tilting her shoulder blades into a curve as she held her head high for all to see how beautiful she was. A young fruit tree with luscious fruits in the thicket of a dark rain forest. Sally sighed. "You too, Glory, why do you look so ripe like this when you are still green, na?" She asked in anguish. Nkongho and Aunty were shocked at this sudden outburst. Sally began to laugh hysterically as her eyes reddened with embarrassment.
"Why are you people looking at me like that? Is she not . ."
"What? Eh, Sally?" Aunty and Nkongho barked at once.
"You this girl, be careful," Aunty warned her. "You don't want me to put a curse on you, beautiful foolish thing."
Nkongho sighed loud and long, then turned and faced her friend.
"Leave my child alone, you hear. It is God who made her so. She looks ripe for people like you who want her to be. Since she is ripe, eat her na?"
Aunty could not believe her ears. "What did you say? Have you all gone crazy?"
Sally ignored her and went on. "If she were a man I would not hesitate."
Nkongho gave her one look and sighed again. "I think there's something wrong with your head. Better go to the hospital for check up."
"Okay, since that's how you see it. I will not open my mouth again," Sally grunted, pouting her lips.

Aunty grabbed Glory's hand, "You these big children, you are so foolish. Let's go, Glory."
Aunty pulled her granddaughter to her side and hailed a taxi. Nkongho and Sally followed suit. As soon as they arrived home they went to Sally's house and celebrated their accomplishment with cold beer. Glory was offered one full bottle all to herself. She would soon be a woman, Aunty explained.

From then on Glory and the rest of Nkongho's children remained indoor all the time, waiting for Nkongho to get all the medical supplies Glory would need in her new condition. Some days she would come home very late with only crepe bandage. Other days she would bring back several bottles of ferrous sulphate. On such days she would explain that she had waited for the doctors and medical superintendent to leave before she could have access to the hospital storeroom. Then Sally had an idea. She hired a taxi and waited out by the clinic gate for her friend to come out with the large bag of clothes they had earlier arranged for Nkongho to take along with her that afternoon. Like other hospital thieves, Nkongho too had to pretend that she was selling clothes. As soon as she showed her head at the door, Sally dashed forward to help her with her load. She gave the night watch man some money for some bottles of beer and the man let her pass without as much as asking them what they had in their large bag.

A week later Sally took Glory to her mother's in the village where she could stay safely until the baby was born. They left one morning as the roosters began crowing but only Sally returned at dusk the following day. She did not utter a word about the trip. All she did was lock eyes with Nkongho and Aunty and smiled before raising a bottle of beer to her lips. They understood as they sipped their own drinks directly from the bottles. That was the end of the matter. To the neighbors Glory had disappeared. She had left the house one day and never returned home. Nkongho would be heard complaining about it night after night, but Mami Nzelle was convinced something was really amiss. She couldn't be fooled. How could a big girl like Glory just disappear like that, she would ask her friends over and over again. But they too were confused. They would sit on the verandah to ponder it all as though it was their business. Then Mami Nzelle would stand up suddenly and shout to Nkongho's hearing that she was a big fat liar. All would be calm again and the women would continue cracking their egusi in silence until such a moment that one of their spouses would return and start shouting for food to be reheated. Only then would they reluctantly go to their different homes and face the reality of their own lives. But Mami Nzelle could still not understand how she had missed Nkongho's new scam as she was quietly referring to it. One day the child was there sitting on the verandah with the others, and the next day she had disappeared leaving her mother and grandmother behind. It wasn't possible. Not Glory! Nkongho's child would not do a thing like that, Mami Nzelle concluded.

Then a year later Glory suddenly appeared looking fresh and strong. Her return was more puzzling than her departure. Mami Nzelle gave up trying to figure out what had really happened. It was none of her business anyway, she quietly consoled herself as she watched the Elates singing and dancing with joy that their daughter had finally returned home in one piece. She had almost accepted defeat and had begun doubting her ability at detecting strange happenings when three months later Sally's Sissy showed up with a plump baby in her care. Sally didn't bother to explain who the baby was. The child resembled nobody. She was just a happy little baby who chuckled all the time as so many different people carried her. Mami Nzelle, Mrs. Sama and the other woman watched on as the baby was constantly being shuffled between Sally's and Nkongho's place. They listened to know who she really was, but no one bothered to explain anything. And the day Sally's mother left the child finally moved in with Nkongho. She became one of her children and that was it. It was then Mami Nzelle noticed a slight resemblance between the child and Nkongho. She remarked about this to her friends who vehemently disagreed with her.

"Ah say, she does look like Nkongho-oh!"

"No, she doesn't even look like any of the other children," the others argued. "Ah, ah Mami Nzelle, were we not here the whole time with Nkongho?"

"She does-eh! Just look at one side of the face, bollo bollo jaws like whose-eh?"

"Then the other side of the face is whose then? Since you know so much." Mrs. Sama stood her grounds.

"You this woman, you are really stupid. How can I know the father when I cannot even figure out who the mother really is? You so, with your long mouth, you can really make someone angry."

The atmosphere became tense. The third woman stared first at Mami Nzelle then at Mrs. Sama and decided not to say what she thought about the issue.

"You call me stupid, eh?"

Mami Nzelle ignored her and cracked the egusi on her tray with such speed and concentration that could make a lazy wife envious.

"Mami Nzelle, you call me stupid just because you don't know the parents of Nkongho's daughter? You are the stupid one," Mrs. Sama said calmly this time.

Mami Nzelle shoved her tray aside.

"What did you say?" She adjusted her wrapper around her waist. "Ah say, what did you say again?" Without waiting for an answer she tossed Mrs. Sama 's egusi on the verandah.

"Get out of here, you woman who doesn't even know the difference between a child that is somebody's and a child that is not somebody's."

Mrs. Sama got up and gathered her egusi from the concrete floor. When she finished, she kicked Mami Nzelle's tray and then walked away singing a song about a dirty woman whose house always had rotten pawpaws that no one liked to eat. Mami Nzelle chased after her but she was too fast to be caught. As all this was happening the other woman sneaked off without a backward glance. Chinyere who had heard and seen everything ran home to relate the story to everyone. Nkongho was immensely pleased. From then on she would take the baby outside with her each time the three women sat on the verandah cracking egusi. She would place the child's face close to hers and smile before returning home to give the women a chance to fight some more; each time they would end up quarreling and calling each other names. It went on like that every day for a week and one day they stopped talking to each other. Each would be seen cracking egusi alone on a separate verandah trying desperately to look happy as they forced their children to hang out with them or play only in their yard where they would be seen. Nkongho stopped flaunting the latest addition to her family. No sooner had she done this for these women to be seen cracking egusi together again on Mami Nzelle's verandah.

Long after everyone had gone to sleep one night and the stars brightened the otherwise plain sky, Mami Nzelle sat on the verandah alone. She had her wrapper fastened across her bosom. Instead of cracking egusi as she usually did, she kept chasing mosquitoes that were buzzing all around her. She had her eyes fixed on her neighbor's house. It stood there as though it would collapse at the slightest wind. It was so fragile that she had hoped it would be swept away by one of those Kumba floods. After all it was a building no one in their right mind would want to occupy. But Nkongho had rented it. Only such a woman could take that kind of a risk with her battalion.

She could hear frogs croaking and a car would screech somewhere in town, but nothing could shake her eyes off this decaying plank house. She heard the baby cry in Nkongho's house. Then she heard Chinyere say it was Enanga's turn to carry the baby. Soon a bed creaked and she could hear footsteps and a lullaby. Minutes later all was fine inside the big plank house. How could an abnormal family be this normal, she thought out loud. Even small Enanga was fast becoming a small mami too. Mami Nzelle sighed and withdrew her eyes away from the clumpsy building that stood beside their concrete house. One last look at the termite infested house she burst into a fit of laughter. "Just like Nkongho, ah tell you true; that house looks like its mother." She felt relieved after saying this. Only then did she get up to retire for the night like everybody else on Krammer Street. As she snuggled under the covers next to her husband who had dozed off, she whispered under her breath that the child was indeed Glory's regardless of what the Elates wanted the world to believe. If only she could find solid proof. Mr. Esag reached for her blindly but his hand found its way under her sweaty armpit. He shoved her away and screamed that she should go take a bath before lying on his nice bed. Moments later he was snoring again. Mami Nzelle took one look at his own sweaty body and turned to face the other side of the wall. The wall that separated them from their kids.

"Nkongho, Elate! Hmm." She mumbled and drifted into a peaceful sleep. She had finally solved the puzzle. She was at peace at last. Or was she as she slept soundly having forgotten about her neighbors' problems momentarily as she rested her enquiring mind that night. At least!

CHAPTER 7

Nkongho and her children had not rested from the past experience when Glory began hanging out with men again. She would be seen laughing coquettishly in the company of hefty men who were old enough to be her father. They came in turns to pick her up right there in the house where she lived with her mother and grandmother. And usually they would come smiling and chatting. Large fancy cars would hoot for her out there by the road side and she would dash out there all dressed up in one ready-made dress after another, and one high heeled shoes after another. Old rickety Renaults would wait for her on other weekends, engine running nonstop and exhaust pipes pouring smoke into the neighborhood air. On such days Glory took her time to walk across the yard to the smoked filled car. And usually she would dress in her Yoruba outfit with a head tie carefully balanced on one side of her head like a dignified wife—a woman married to a financially strapped man who is trying to hold his own too against all odds. Brand new Mercedes stopped for her also occasionally; Volvos and even yellow taxis that had been hired to take her somewhere to meet with someone who does not want to be seen with her in public. Those rich men who like to go to the gutter for their thrills but would not admit it in public. Yes, they all came for Glory. She glowed with pride.

One evening as she took her time dressing up for one of her wretched customers, the driver sat in the old Volvo purring endlessly. This time Mami Nzelle had had it. She strolled over and told the man off. Krammer, she reminded him, was a very respectable neighborhood. The man smiled and looked away pressing more gas to keep his engine running.

"You can turn your face anyhow you want, but I don't want you to think that all the girls here are like that one over there," she said pointing at Glory who was already approaching the noisy car.
"You hear me?"
"Yes, Madam," the driver replied calmly
"Okay, Now you can leave. Oya, go."
The man gave her a quizzical look.
"Ah say, you can leave now."
Instead he stopped the engine and came out of the car.
"Madam," he began. "You do not understand."
Mami Nzelle looked at him from head to toe and cupped her mouth with her hand.
"What don't you understand, eh, you small boy for yesterday?" She looked around for support but everybody else was minding her own business.
"What don't you understand, you thief man? And where did you get the money for even buy this ekete Volvo sef?" She kicked the side of the car.
"Madam, no do so, ah beg you. Oga will not like it. My oga..." he started to explain.
"Patrick!"
"Yes, Madam." He stood up straight and waited for further instructions from Glory.
"What's this?" Mami Nzelle, hands akimbo shouted.
Patrick ignored her and simply opened the door to the backseat for Glory. All dressed up in door blind lace this time, she adjusted her buttocks on the seat and carefully spread out the surplus cheap lace material on the rest of the seat. With dark glasses hanging on her nose she took one look at a confused Mami Nzelle and told her to go service her husband before she came and showed her how a man can be serviced. At that her Volvo drove off pouring more smoke and dust this time in the air. Mami Nzelle opened her mouth to say something but almost choked. She ran home coughing and cussing first at Glory and Nkongho; after catching her breath she cussed all the idle young women who spent nights in chicken parlors and fancy hotels.

Glory was on top of her game, looking fresher and fresher every day in the company of men who took her to Play Fair or Hotel Authentic or to nice neighboring towns like Victoria or Douala. Weekend after weekend in different hotels and guesthouses, she was the envy of her peers. She changed dresses and shoes as though she merely picked them from the streets. At first, Aunty was impressed.

But then when they could no longer recognize some of the men Aunty became worried and told her so. Nothing changed.

Her mother didn't know what to do, but her brothers did. Jacob and Simon beat her up. She was too much of a disgrace they later confided to their mother. Glory in turn, starved them for two whole days. She said she wasn't going to cook for people who were jealous because she was enjoying her youth. Jacob beat her up again. This time, in addition to starving him, she confiscated their only bed sheet, saying it used to be her school sheet. Jacob and Simon didn't mind sleeping on a bare mattress, especially since Jacob now spent most of his time at his shed in the market. He was busy making money to support the others through secondary schools. The likes like Glory who kept failing one exam after another. He had clearly told their mother that if Glory failed G.C.E one more time he would stop wasting his hard earned money on her. They all thought he was joking until one such day when he actually stopped helping out with Glory's fees. Only then did Nkongko acknowledge that he was a tough boy who meant business. And sometimes she wondered if that wasn't the reason why Glory openly misbehaved with those her men. If it was the reason Jacob didn't care. He had to put his feet down as he later explained to their mother. Or else all their money would be spent only on one child who wasn't even grateful. Their mother saw with him and advised her daughter to stop wasting her time writing the ordinary level exam. Glory got mad and threatened to move out and go where they would let her write her exams in peace. Jacob said she was just a stupid whore who wanted her freedom to live as she pleased. This was too much for Glory who took a mortar pestle and began hitting her younger brother anywhere it landed. In turn, Jacob elbowed her, then hooked her head in the curve of his arm and began pressing until such a time that she was screaming and pleading for mercy. Only then did he let her go. From then on she went out whenever she liked and returned as it pleased her. When her mother asked her why she was behaving like that she asked her to stay out of her business. She was above Aunty too.

Night after night Aunty, Nkongho and Sally sat on the verandah to wait up for her. When she returned she would pass as though she had not seen them and went to sleep without asking for supper. Aunty would throw her hands up in the air and swear in their dialect. She would ask herself several times what her ancestors had done to deserve such punishment. At the end of such ramblings she would sigh and shake her head from side to side, feeling sorry for her daughter. That was usually the cue for Nkongho to support her. Both women would sigh for hours while Sally remained silent. It was beyond her understanding why a young girl would insist on perpetually disgracing the family name like that. But

one day she spoke out. "Epo, this your own child like this pass me-oh. Honestly, I give up." After letting this out she realized she had blundered.
"Look at who is talking too," Aunty sneered. "Are all children not more than you to raise?"
Sally got mad. "At least, my children are being raised properly."
Nkongho gave her friend another look. This look sent Sally running to her beautiful home where peace forever reigned.

As Glory continued with this bad behavior the rest of the family held a meeting to decide her fate. They did this in secret, so the neighbors would not have the slightest clue as to how Glory's attitude was affecting them. The older boys suggested she looked for a job and a place of her own so she wouldn't be a bad influence on the others. When they told her this, Glory said she wasn't ready for a job yet. Her classmates were still students, even though some were working on their Advanced levels and others were at the university. She would not become a worker that early. Fed up with this attitude, Nkongho asked her to join her brothers in the market. Glory would have none of it. Did they see her like a market girl? Was she that desperate, she shouted into her mother's face. When Jacob insisted that she joined them, she told him she would never, because her father would never approve of that line of business for her. Her father, she reminded them came from a place where people worked for a living but in an office and not in makeshift sheds like sufferers. This troubled Simon so much that he stopped helping his brother in the market. He said it was time he also went back to school. But his real brother, Jacob would have none of that rubbish. Their future was in that market he reminded them repeatedly. Still Simon was not convinced. Their mother begged him to give it another thought. He said he was quite certain education was what he wanted now.
He hung around the house for a month sorting out the books that would be useful for the first form he intended to start soon. It was easy to do that, for their mother had carefully stored all the left over books in an old trunk. He found a few and picked out one that caught his fancy. On flipping through this textbook he saw Monday's name on all the sides, then James' on the front page, and finally Chinyere's in the middle of the book. The only constant was the last name Elate. On the page where Chinyere had written her name, there was an arrow pointing to where the next owner should put his or her name. That instant it occurred to him that the next in line would really be Enanga. Only then did he give up the idea of returning to school. It was for children, he later confided in his mother.

Back with his older brother in the market the issue of Glory's lifestyle came up again as they sought for a proper way to deal with it. Acting on their mother's advice they gave her one more chance to decide whether she was getting a job or not, but Glory remained adamant. Jacob stopped coming to the house. He said he would only come there when Glory had changed her bad behavior. Together with Simon they stopped paying Enanga's fees. It was her sister's responsibility to help with the child, they told Nkongho. Enanga stopped looking after Catherine. She told Glory that she wouldn't work on credit anymore. Glory reminded her then that as her real sister it was her responsibility to help out with the child. Chinyere said it was not true. Glory argued that it was. Enanga took sides with her real sister. Much as she hated it she became the only person looking after Catherine. Some times when Glory forced her to do so, she would pinch the child on the buttocks until Catherine would flee from her care.

The family was in crisis all because of Glory. The older boys stayed away more often and some days they didn't even bother to show up for their supper. Jacob showed up one morning before their mother could leave for work and told her that he and Simon planned to move out. Nkongho burst into tears and skipped work that day. Her family was falling apart right in front of her own eyes. Weh, what would she do-eh? She was still dealing with this when Simon came in and started packing their belongings. Nkongho cried some more. For an entire week the boys kept reminding her about their eminent departure. As all these went on in the house Aunty remained silent. At times, she would clap her hands in wonder. Glory, she finally told Nkongho one night, must look for a job and start helping more like the others. It was Nkongho's place to impart this firmly into her daughter's head. Nkongho said she did not know how to tell her child to work. Aunty grabbed her by the wrist. "Have you ever heard of a mother being afraid of her own flesh and blood, eh, you this weakling of a woman? Tell her she has to look for a job. She is not a student; she is not married; she is not working; what is she? Epo, what is your daughter?"

"Why don't you ask her yourself, eh? Are you not her grandmother?" Nkongho replied pulling her arm away from the older woman's clutch.

"Okay, if that is what you want, I'll do it."

"Fine. Do it let somebody drink water in this house again. War, war, war every day! What's wrong with having a little peace for a change?"

"Ask me again, you woman who doesn't know the difference between an owner and a tourist."

Nkongho could not believe her ears. She stared at her mother with burning eyes then clapped her hands in wonder. At that moment she hated that woman even more than she loathed her own life. "Aunty," she began calmly controlling herself, "Don't make me abuse you too. You, who knows the difference, where is your own owner? Eh?"

"Don't you even dare open your mouth and talk to me like that, Epo. You know that I can curse you, not so?"

"You wouldn't dare?"

"Just try me. You and your children should be very careful. That your Glory so, if I pin my feet on her back she will be sorry," Aunty threatened.

"Just leave them alone. They are mine and not yours," she said defeatedly.

"I know that. But she has to get a job before we lose those boys."

Like Aunty said, Glory had to get a job. She had no choice in the matter anymore. Nkongho tried the hospital but there was nothing else her daughter could do there that didn't require ordinary level certificate. She tried some shops in town and a few restaurants all in vain. She was almost giving up when Sally found something. It was a receptionist job at a hotel. Sally explained that all Glory had to do was smile and act nice. Anybody could do that, even Glory! Besides, one didn't need a certificate for such a job. Glory did not fail to show up for work the first day as the three older women had feared.

The moment she started working Jacob stopped sleeping in the shed and life returned to normal. Then Monday started his own trouble too. He said he was tired of being a day student and would want to stay in the dormitory like most of his classmates. At first, no one took him seriously. James told him outright that he was a selfish boy. Chinyere just wondered at such arrogance; Jacob and Glory would have none of that nonsense in their house. Then he asked why Sister Glory had stayed in the dormitory while they were struggling as day students. Nkongho was stunned at this sudden outburst from the son who never complained. She told him to shut up and he got even madder and said it was because Glory was the daughter of her favorite man. Glory backhanded him across the face. "Stop that rubbish at once!" He charged forward toward her and she gave him another. "I am working everyday to take care of you people and you can't even be grateful," she yelled at him. Monday stared at his sister in disbelief. Unable to control himself anymore, he pounced on her and began kicking and boxing her stomach. Jacob and Simon dragged him away as Glory also started clawing his face.

"Are you out of your mind, eh, you this Monday?" Jacob scolded. "Since when did you start fighting with Glory? Do you know that she's the one who gave you your first enema? She's a second mother to you, do you know that, eh, you this swine?" Jacob kicked him on the buttocks and began spanking him across the face.

"I am a swine; what are you? She is Bakweri. Ask Sister Nkongho if she even cared about our own father. Just ask her before you kill your own real brother," Monday pleaded as tears flowed down his oily cheeks.
"I am Bakweri and so are you. Look at you crying like little Catherine. You are not even ashamed sef. What if you were James and Chinyere, eh?"
"Brother Jacob, what is wrong with us, eh?" Chinyere fired back.
"Nothing, and you shut your mouth up," Jacob barked at his younger sister at the same time turning to face his real brother. "Monday, have you thought about Simon? After class seven did you see him go to college like you people? He is with me day in, day out in the market. Have you heard us complain? Eh? Answer me. That's how children like you who don't work money are ungrateful. I have the good mind to eat my money alone."
"Papa, leave it like that, ah beg you."
"No, Aunty, I have to speak out. It is too much. They are Sister's children and not Sister Glory's and mine. We are helping because we are kind. The bagga thinks that it is his right."
"Jacob, leave my son alone. He has every right to want to stay in the dormitory too. So leave him alone!"
"Then you look after him yourself, Sister Nkongho. Don't ever ask us for help again."
"Yes, I will. You and Glory are too much. Why do you help a child and then turn your back and insult him? Eh? Was it not Sally who gave you the capital to start your own business? Has she turned her back and insulted you?"
"Brother Jack, what did my brother and I do to you too?" Chinyere demanded again.
"Shut up!" Glory, Jacob and Nkongho barked at her. Like lightning, Chinyere turned around and slapped Enanga.
"Stop that at once, you palaver finder," Aunty screamed.
"Epo, hold that your crazy child before she kills our real child."
Chinyere burst into tears. "Aunty, how can you too say that, na? I am glad even. Ashawos."
Enanga bit her and tried to run away but Chinyere cornered her and kicked her hard on her behind. She started crying. Glory, who had gone to the room to change her clothes, rushed into the room and attacked Chinyere. James joined in. "Leave my sister alone, you good for nothing daughter of a drunkard." He jumped on her.
"Get off my back you young Biafran. Get off me before I show you something." They made so much raucous that the neighbors gathered around to see what was

happening. Mami Nzelle ran as fast as she could to see for herself. But Sally was faster. Once she arrived she bolted the door from inside and shut the windows. Then she joined Nkongho, Aunty and Jacob who were busy trying to stop the fight. Monday sat on a chair at the far end of the parlor unperturbed. Simon escaped through the back window.

By evening all had calmed down in the huge dilapidated plank house inhabited by Nkongho and her family. But Mami Nzelle, Mrs. Sama and the other woman could not really understand what had happened.

"Who was fighting with who-eh?" she kept asking.

"I don't know-oh. But it was something about money," Mrs. Sama replied.

"No. Somebody said 'don't slap my sister;' another said 'don't beat my brother.' Are they not all Nkongho's children?" the other woman asked.

"Of course, you fool. Have you seen a man in there?"

"I was just asking, na."

"How can you ask such a question even?" Mrs. Sama snapped.

"Okay, I won't put my mouth there again."

This seemed to put an end to their conversation that evening. It was just as well, for out of the blue it began to rain. They dispersed early.

In her big three bedroom house all by herself, Sally just clapped her hands in wonder. She thought she had problems, but Nkongho's, hmmm! This was all she could say.

It was a long night at the Elates as none had had supper that evening simply because no one had been willing to cook. The children had all gone to bed angry with one another. Their stomachs growled and gnawed at the same time as each tried hard to sleep. It was futile to blame the noise coming from their bellies on hunger. They had not cooked, so there was nothing to eat. Not even garri to soak and eat, for that was what Aunty and Catherine had had. The rain beat hard on their rusty roof and every once in a while Nkongho would get up and check the rooms to make sure that buckets and enamel basins had been placed under the leaky spots. She could feel the force of the wind slamming neighboring doors and occasionally her house seemed to be shaking. It was thundering out there like she had never seen since she moved into Krammer Street. It was as though nature was at war with itself. Lightning would flash across the sky, followed by loud thundering and more rain would pour down washing the ground on the foundation of her rented house. Nkongho sat alone in the parlor and watched this display of wrath. The forces of nature seemed to be fighting against each other and yet they had no choice but to share the sky they each operated from. At that moment, Nkongho felt the heavy load of being the mother of all her children, including little Catherine. She could feel the load on her shoulders as she tried to get up and return to the room. She tried to stand up but was unable to. It seemed like someone with strong hands was pushing her back to the chair. She tried one more time and gave up. Instead, she raised her knees under her long nightgown to fit in the narrow cushioned chair. She began to doze off in this position but was awakened by a cry from the boys' room. With all her might she hauled herself out of that chair and walked slowly to see what had happened. It was Monday. He said he was too hungry to sleep. He sat there crying like an orphan. Under normal circumstances Nkongho would have asked him to go out there in the rain and fix something to eat, but she did not. She defied the rain and went to the kitchen to scramble an egg for her son. It wasn't much but it soothed him to sleep. She sat on the floor in the boys' room until the next morning without as much as closing her eyes.

Jacob felt sorry for her when he got up early to prepare for work the next day. He hugged her and told her ashia before leaving. Nkongho smiled and patted her son on the back. "Thank you, Papa."

He grinned.

It was her life and they were her children. It was her privilege to look after them without complaining. After all, wasn't she the one who had brought them into this world? So like the mother she was, she mustered courage to prepare for work herself. Nkongho grabbed a towel, wrapper and a bucket and headed for the bathroom. As usual half way there she stopped to get some water from the well. It was a tedious morning as she toiled over the over flooded well to pull just one bucket of water to wash off the night's strain. The first pail she dragged looked cloudy. She threw that on someone's garden and waited for clay to settle down in the cradle of the deep hole that generously supplied them with water. She tried again; this time it wasn't as cloudy, but it had a faint odor. She sighed and carried her bucket of water away. Then she noticed a pile of sticks and sheets of zinc crumpled on the ground where her private bathroom had been standing. Her limbs went weak and she let go of the cleanest water she had been able to get out of the well not too long ago. It flowed gently away as it slowly mingled with the mushy surrounding to create a haven for more mosquitoes. Nkongho made an about turn to get some more water. This time she went but to the pit latrine her children normally used and took a quick bath, holding her breath through the long five minutes. It was only on her way back to the main house that she noticed something about the guava tree. It looked kind of bare, as the night storm had shamelessly ravished two of its branches. Nkongho sighed again. She stood there for some minutes and took in the entire scene. The tree looked helpless under the seemingly bright sky with the ground around its trunk completely washed away revealing the harder surface—the core—that firmly anchored its roots. Only people didn't really notice this. Nkongho saw some children running toward it. They kept saying 'weh, weh' as they hastily examined the damages caused by the night's storm. As soon as they began gathering stones to support these branches from completely falling off Nkongho walked away to do what she also must do if her family should continue to stay afloat. She went to work.

CHAPTER 8

Nkongho's problems multiplied. She wished that life would pause briefly so she could sort things out. It went on anyway. The children had stopped talking with one another. It was now one full week. She really needed time to wait; may be just a minute. Aunty ignored them and concentrated on Enanga and Catherine. Then one day Glory brought home some roasted chicken a customer had graciously offered her. They feasted on this and became a family once more. Aunty just smiled and was happy that she could now live a normal life.

Not long after this, they saw a jeep toiled its way through the slippery road until it arrived its destination, Sally's house. A young woman in her early twenties, dressed in a brown leather skirt and white silk blouse pushed her high-heeled shoes out. Her entire body followed after as she stretched out of the jeep and brushed a wrinkle from her skirt. She swung her shoulder bag around her fingers brushing locks of permed hair off her neck. She looked really sophisticated like one of those "been tos" who took their time to get tropicalized. She knitted her eyebrows then smiled at no one in particular. A group of boys whistled at her and she burst out laughing. She was indeed beautiful. Her kind of beauty was a gift, not the kind merely bought by money the way rich people did. Of course, hers might have been accentuated by the easy life she might have led or still be living.

She stood by the side of the road for a minute and watched the boys disappear. The smile disappeared as she sized up the neighborhood. Nothing had changed since her last visit, which was a long time ago. She really could not remember how long ago that was. Krammer remained the filthy place she had loathed and would continue to not like. Only then did she haul her suitcase and beckoned to the driver to take care of the flour bag of accessories she had carefully brought from Yaounde. It contained all the relevant items her father believed she would need to survive in the jungle where her mother lived. It was the only way he would let her visit that woman. A good compromise that suited Elsie only too well.

Across the street Mami Nzelle and her friends watched the new woman. Elsie pulled up her skirt and jumped over the narrow gutter that separated Sally's house and the road. Sally's houseboy saw her and immediately ran to help. He said something to the woman and pointed toward the fragile plank house on the other side of the street. She wrinkled her nose and gazed at the direction briefly. Nkongho and her family were in their own house laughing at a joke Chinyere had cracked when they heard a knock and a tall, slim woman appeared like an apparition in the doorway. She barely spoke as she stood there scrutinizing the people who were supposed to be her mother's best friends. The Elates ignored her too. Then Chinyere dropped her ruler and pencil on the table and looked at this woman straight in the eyes and asked her what she wanted.

"Sally," Elsie replied.

"Oh, why didn't you just say so?" Chinyere stood up with a broad smile on her face. "Sit down too and let me get her for you. She is in the room." Chinyere offered her chair to the guest. Glory, Nkongho and Aunty cast one glance at this person and took their eyes away as they concentrated once more on the koki beans they were peeling for that evening's supper. Sally came out adjusting her wrapper around her waist.

"Yes?"

"It's me."

"You, who?" She fixed her eyes on the young woman's legs and gradually moved them up to her smooth pear shaped face. Her eyes lit up. "Oh, my God!" She embraced her.

"Oh, my God. It is my very own Elsie. Fine pickin all grown up!" She queezed her tight in a warm embrace. "Oh, my child. You've grown-oh! You don big-oh!"

Elsie nodded.

"You be woman now-oh. Turn around let me see your small waist now."

Elsie stood still.

"Look at my child, Epo." She placed both hands on Elsie's shoulder to display the fine specimen of a child she had produced. "My very own daughter from the capital city. Everybody, my daughter, Elsie."

"Is that why she cannot greet people?" Aunty grunted.

"Ah, ah you too, Aunty. She is just a child!"

"Welcome then Sally's child," they greeted Elsie.

"Let's go to the house, my child," Sally said extending a hand to her daughter without showing the slightest indication that her friends' attitude bothered her. "How is your brother, na? Is he well? How is Yaounde? Weh, boh."

No sooner had they left than for someone else to knock on Nkongho's door. Chinyere stood up. "I hope it's not Sally and that her child again. Who is it?" she barked. Instead of an answer, a tall, plump man whose face could do with some shaving cream and razor pushed his way in.

"And now what is it you want?" Glory asked.

He grinned and shoved the girl out of his face. "Is that how you people welcome strangers in your house? Do you know that I could be one of your fathers?"

"So?"

"Greet me well then."

"If you missed your way just turn back and go the way you came. We have enough problems as it is," Glory said adjusting her buttocks on a cushioned chair.

The man lost his temper. "Is this a house even? Holes, holes everywhere when everybody now is staying in a block house." He walked toward Glory and shoved her head. "You, like this with your long mouth. You must be Glory, or is it Efeti? You are just like Aunty. Always talk, talk insult people. Stand up and go get my bag before I join you all and beat like foofoo."

Aunty froze in her seat. Nkongho got up and marched forward. She had paid every single coin of her rent and would not let any man just walk in there and tell them off like that. "Now, what do you want? And leave my children alone!"

He chuckled. "You know what I want. I want Glory. Isn't that what she does now or do you think I don't know?"

"Take your bad luck and get out of my house."

"Make me."

"Monday, go to the market and call your brothers let them come this instant." The child started to leave.

"Oh, no, Monday, you will not do anything of that sort," the stranger barred the doorway.

"Okay," Monday said simply and went back into their room.

"Epo, you and your mother are not even ashamed sef. Aunty, you too can't recognize me? All these years I'm in Calabar thinking of the big welcome that I'll receive from my family. You people are really something!" He shrugged his shoulders and backed away from the door. "Well, I have your news, Epo." At that moment, Monday retraced his steps and dashed into his arms. "Uncle," he called out excitedly.

"Nice, but tough." The older man caught the young boy and hugged him tightly closing his eyes at each squeeze.
"Thank you, my son."
"Weh, Uncle. Welcome."
"Thank you, my son," he said again opening his eyes that were already clouded with tears.
"Jerome," Aunty began but could not go further as tears welled in her eyes. "My child, are these your eyes? All these hundred of years, where have you been? You abandoned me that who will look after me? Eh, my son?" She began sobbing.
"Aunty, don't start that now. It is not me who told you not to marry." Letting Monday go, he looked around and shook his head. "I see your Epo has wisely taken after you. How nice!"
"Don't you comment about my life-eh. If you were a good brother, wouldn't you have helped me look for a man? Besides, where is your own wife?"
"None of your bloody business. And you, Aunty, how have you been?" He walked over and enveloped his mother in a long embrace.
"My life would have been better if you were somebody," she retorted struggling not to need the hug.
"Okay, I've heard."
Chinyere and Glory didn't know what to make of this. They listened to their grandmother, mother and uncle blame each other for their lives until Chinyere began telling her sister that she would marry, even if it meant marrying a poor man. Glory laughed at her and said she would continue searching until she found someone like Elsie's father. The kind that not only had money, but also a Masters degree. Chinyere thought she was aiming too high, but Glory would not step down from high horse. So the discussion ended with neither of them agreeing on the right path to take. They went to the market later and announced uncle's arrival to their brothers.

That evening it was a family meeting like none they had ever had. Uncle Jerome brought out a sack of clothes for James and Chinyere. He said it was what their father, whom he had succeeded to locate in another part of the country, could send for the moment. He said Monday's father had sent them a carton of books, which he had left at his girl friend's. That same evening Jacob accompanied him to collect the carton. For once the boy felt like somebody too as they drove in the taxi his uncle had cleverly chartered for the day.

Jerome told them stories about Lagos, Enugu, Onitsha, Calabar and other towns and places that meant nothing to them. He said he had a law firm in Calabar. He emphasized that as a lawyer his life was pretty good. As proof, he would toss a few nairas in their faces to show how successful he truly was. It didn't take long for the word to spread around, and before people knew it he was seen driving around town in one borrowed car after another with Sally's daughter by his side. Sally didn't approve and she told Nkongho so. Nkongho in turn warned her brother to drop the girl, but he would not listen. They were in love, he told her. Nkongho washed her hands off their business. But Sally would not accept that nonsense. She complained repeatedly to Nkongho until one day Aunty told her not to bother them again with her problem. Sally lost her temper and told them off.

"Your son is a beast. Just look at my Elsie."

They ignored her.

"If he doesn't leave her alone I am going to call the police."

Aunty took one look at Sally and ordered her out of their house. The woman refused to leave. She wasn't leaving until they assured her that they would put an end to the rubbish.

"Suit yourself then." Aunty got up to leave the parlor.

"Aunty, ah serious-oh. You people should tell me what kind of love portion you've fed my child. Jerome should be hanging out with girls like Glory. Not my Elsie." She sighed and folded her arms across her bosom.

"What did you say?" Nkongho jumped out of her seat.

"Sister, why do you ask that? Just make her tell us exactly what kind of a girl I am."

Sally sighed again. "You don't want to know. You people are afraid of the truth, and the truth is that he is not good enough for my daughter. I've said it, if you people care, come and kill me."

"You are not even ashamed to say that, you this Sister Sally. Do you even have a child? Eh?" Glory added.

"Yes, you sit there and open your dirty mouth as though you know what it really means to have a child. You there, what is your child's favorite food? My Glory here likes plantains best. What does your Elsie eat?"

"I will not sit in this dirty house and receive insults from people like you. Epo, see your house, see your children and you call yourself a professional. Nurse, my foot!"

"Ashawo!" Glory screamed at her.

Sally froze on the spot where she stood. "What did you call me?"

"I said, 'Ashawo,' go and hang."

"A badly brought up child like you call me what? Look at your mother, what do you see? Look at yourself, what do you see? Do you even have a father? And you have the nerve to call me an ashawo? Make God punish you for your ingratitude. You so, you be witch."

Nkongho slapped her. She slapped Nkongho back. A big fight broke out right there in Nkongho's parlor. Nkongho and Glory slapped and boxed her on different parts of the body. Sally fought back too as she yelled out more insults. When Nkongho and her daughter finally pinned her on the ground they dealt one last blow on her jaw that brought out blood. Only then did they leave her and wiped their hands on their partly torn dresses.

"Now you can get out of our dirty house before my children who don't have fathers kill you." Sally staggered to the door.

"You this Nkongho, I always knew you were a bad woman. You so, who carries it in the hand and distributes it to any Tom, Dick and Harry."

"Get out quickly." Nkongho kicked her. She stumbled on to the verandah.

"Kick me all you want, it wouldn't change the fact that you have brought lots of sufferers into this world. You woman weh i no know how to say 'no.'"

Glory pounced on her out there and began hitting her again. Aunty who was in the room all this while came out and pulled Glory off Sally. She dragged her in and slammed the door shut. Mami Nzelle and her friends were already at the scene watching and whispering. Sally paid no heed to them. She went on, "Epo, even if you and your battalion kill me, my daughter will not be seen with a man who is not from a regular family. You people have forgotten who her father is. Not poor church rats like yours!" She paused to take a long breath. "As God is my witness, my little Elsie will not err like that! She has too much training."

"Carry your bad luck and go away." Chinyere shouted from behind the door. Mami Nzelle grabbed Sally, as she was about to throw stones at the plank house.

"Don't do it, Sally. They will kill you, my sister. You don't know this kind of people-oh."

"Yes, I do and they will not reduce my well-brought up child to their level. No! I don't want bad blood in my family. What will Simon say? Eh, Mami Nzelle? That I can't even provide a safe environment for my own flesh and blood?"

"He will not say that, my sister. This your Simon, whoever he is will not think you are a bad woman. You don't even bring your own men to your house sef?"

"What?" Sally screamed, freeing her arm from this woman who had been trying to reason with her. "You just take your own bad luck and go away. Just go. Go give your man food or something. Isn't that what you married women do? Go."

"What did I do wrong, na?"

"Just go with your bad luck." Sally said one last time and headed home to nurse her wounds. Once there, she packed her daughter's things and waited for her to return. When she did Sally told her to go back to her father where it was far much safer. Elsie refused. She said she was tired of living with her father and his wicked wife. They had tortured her enough. Sally burst into fresh tears asking God why He was punishing her like that. Tears or not Elsie would not change her ways; neither would she leave.

Six weeks later things changed. One neighbor came to the off License and said Jerome had suddenly left for Lagos. To make matters worse, Elsie missed her period. When she broke the news to her mother Sally sobbed uncontrollably for hours and cursed her ancestors for perhaps not washing her path well.

"How can a good girl like you disgrace herself like that, eh, Elsie?"

"I don't know, Sister."

"Now your father will think I am a bad woman. Your brother too. Weh." Fresh tears streamed down her cheeks.

"He already thinks you are bad."

"Eh? My son?"

Elsie nodded. Sally dried her tears and thought for a little while.

"Was Jerome your first?" After saying this she felt foolish and brushed it aside.

"I really don't know why I said that. Weh, my daughter." Then she stared at the beautiful young woman by her side and shook her head in disbelief.

"He must be or else you were already bad at your father's."

At the possibility of this thought she jumped up and started singing songs of praise. Her daughter had already been bad at her father's.

"Just leave me alone with your questions. So I'm a bad girl, should I go kill myself?" Elsie too began sobbing. "I can't go to Yaounde like this. Daddy will kill me."

Sally's momentary joy was sapped out of her system and she joined her daughter in mourning the loss of her good name. The two women wept the entire night. It was only the next day when they heard the siren of an ambulance that Sally thought of a way to restore her daughter back to normal. She acted fast and soon all was fine again. As soon as Elsie was strong, Sally sent her back to her father without anyone suspecting what had happened. Thank goodness she had taken care of the damage or else she too would have become the laughing stock of Krammer Street. The next couple of weeks she stayed in door to enjoy her peace. It felt good to not worry about what she would have had to explain to her daughter's father if anything bad had happened to his child. The noise from the bar did not bother her one bit. Neither did it soothe her. She lay on her couch day in, day out only in a wrapper and a bra thanking her good fortunes. And the weeks dragged by. Just like that.

Then three full months later Aunty dropped by. Without uttering a word she made space for the older woman on the couch and eventually got up to serve her something. As Aunty quietly washed down bowls of tasty pepper soup and bush meat with bottles of cold beer, which Sally had so generously set in front of her, the younger woman sobbed. Aunty ignored her and continued chewing her bush meat with relish and drank more beer.

'Good pepper soup," she grunted. These were things she had missed the most when they were not talking to one another. Aunty took one look at her and threw her face elsewhere. When she finished eating her sumptuous meal she got up to leave.

"Sally," she began then belched. "You know what you need right now?"

She waited for a response, but when none came she carried on.

"Really, my child, it is your mother you need now. Go to her and rest a little."

"You don't understand, Aunty. My Sissy has already developed high blood pressure. I don't want it to get worse."

Aunty looked away. Sally continued sobbing. "I don't know what to do now that even my daughter, Glory will not talk to me too." She blew her nose. "Sit, na Aunty."

The older woman hesitated before returning to her seat. Sally hiccupped.

"See Aunty, the other day Chinyere threw water outside when she saw me passing; as for Jacob and his brothers, it is as if I'm invisible to them. What should I do now, Aunty?"

Aunty got up again and went to the bathroom and when she returned she refused to sit back in the upholstered couch she loved so much. Instead, she stared at Sally's tearstained face and sighed. "Sally, Epo is your friend. Go and talk to her. She has children too, you know? They may be bad but they are hers all the same."

"Weh, Aunty, how can you talk like that na?"

"My child, what do you want me to say? That I forgive you for calling my own flesh and blood bad?" She chuckled. "Okay, I forgive you, but go and see Epo and settle this thing with her." She opened the front door to leave instead of the side door she usually used in the past.

"Aunty, ask the boy to give you some beer to take home with you," Sally offered in a desperate attempt to make peace. Aunty shook her head against that. "Epo is my daughter," she paused. "Sally, my only daughter! You are a good child too, but I can't take your beer to her house until you two have settled your problem."

With that she walked out of the building that was booming as ever with all types of customers. Right behind her was Sally.

She followed the older woman to Nkongho's house but hesitated to enter the parlor. Aunty left her standing there and joined her family. When Sally worked up the courage to knock on the door there was no 'who is there?' Just sighs and curses from inside the house. Despite this she showed her face looking meek. Nkongho sighed again; Glory and Chinyere cracked their egusi without acknowledging her presence. Sally coughed, then smiled.

"Aunty, can I come in?" She stammered.

"This is not my house," Aunty answered.

"Glory, can I come in?" Sally asked sheepishly.

"I am just a badly brought up child leaving in a terrible house."

"Ah, ah, you too."

"She is right," Chinyere jumped in. "Our house is not good enough for rich people." Sally stood by the door for a few minutes feeling stupid. Unable to make herself beg, she turned round and walked away. Nkongho and her children burst out laughing.

"Epo," Aunty began, "she offered me beer."

"I see."

"But I didn't take it. You are my daughter."

"I know, Aunty."

"Now, you buy me beer."

"All right, Aunty," Nkongho replied, standing up to get some money from her purse. She gave this to her daughter, Enanga and told her to buy it from a different Off License. The girl did just that.

"Epo, you didn't have to do that."

"Yes, Aunty, I have to teach her some sense."

"She is a good child."

"Yes, but we are not good enough for her."

"You should be more forgiving. After all she is a year or two younger."

Nkongho gave Aunty a nasty look that said it all.

"Did I tell you that I was older? We are both the same age; just that she looks like a girl."

"Okay," Aunty persisted, "but you are a mother of many children and she has really helped you. Do not forget that."

"All right, Aunty."

"You aged faster than your brother," Aunty said as an afterthought. "Can you believe he still looked thirty-something?"

Glory and Chinyere laughed. "He fooled our queen's daughter. God really saved her; she would have had an old man's child," Glory remarked absentmindedly. All eyes turned toward her.

"Don't look at me like that. Catherine is not an old man's daughter. She is his son's and the boy will soon graduate from the university with a Matrise in something!

"Heh?" Nkongho and Aunty exclaimed simultaneously.

"Yes," Glory replied beaming.

"Glory, do you think that was wise?" Nkongho asked anxiously.

"Ah, ah, you too, Sister. Is Cata not here with us? You worry too much."

"Epo, the child did the best thing at the time. Leave her alone. At least, she chose correct people to misbehave with; not like you or that Sally's stupid daughter."

"Oh, Aunty!" Nkongho said simply. "Glory, you so, we shall hear your news."

Chinyere felt a surge of anger building within her. She had this sudden urge to punch her sister's face as Glory sat there shamelessly bragging about her misdeeds. She burst out, "Sister Glory, you so, you are the real ashawo. A big one." She made for the door but her mother restrained her.

"When you wear those hand-me-down expensive ready-made clothes, where do you think I get them from, eh, Virgin Mary? Or you think I get them all from our next door queen, eh?"

"Just leave me alone. You like this, you will scare off all the potential suitors with your bad fashion. You don't realize that you are spoiling my road too."

"Stop it at once, Chinyere! Has she not tried for you, eh?"

"You people are all the same, James was right. That's why our Papa could not marry you. Cameroon bitches."

"Are you out of your mind, Chinyere?"

"Aunty, you leave me alone. I'm tired of all this suffer life." She made for the door.

"Chinyere, don't leave this room until you apologize to your big sister."

Chinyere returned to her seat and began sobbing. At that moment, Sally pushed the door blind aside and stepped in with a basket of cooked food in her expensive breakable dishes. She placed this on the table, stepped out and brought in a crate of sweet drinks. By nightfall the problem she had with the Elates was forgotten as they all laughed and chatted loudly like old times. A month later she asked Chinyere to move in with her. The girl did happily and saved herself the embarrassment of watching her sister being picked up night after night by different men. But this was just one problem that the Elates had finally solved, or believed they had handled well. Aunty thanked her good fortunes too and waited.

Nkongho also waited. They were always waiting for something to go wrong and indeed something finally happened.

CHAPTER 9

Monday failed his exams and was told to repeat the form again. Repeat again were the most awful words at that moment. It wouldn't have been so awful if his younger brother, James had not been promoted to that same class. Worse yet, James did ten subjects while Monday struggled with six. James was the smart one, Monday was the strong one, their mother had said. But the children didn't think this was funny. Chinyere was a class behind them. Any carelessness on their part she would be in the same class with them also. They didn't want that to happen. So the boys took to serious studying. This diverted their attention a bit from what their big sister was doing with her own life. To ease their studying Sally offered her pantry as their reading room, but the two boys must return home after their study sessions each night. It didn't matter how late it was, for she didn't want so many people in her house all the time. At first, it was fun as they consumed book after book without the slightest disturbance from anybody. Then it became an obsession as they noticed Chinyere reading for a much longer period without rest than them. Monday got mad and hid some of the girl's textbooks. Suspecting that the boys might have had a hand in the disappearance of her book, she hid theirs too. Then hers suddenly appeared. She handed over theirs without any explanation. It was like this all the time. But it was better than studying in their house. There they risked hearing about Sister Glory's escapades with men, which reminded them of how different their family was from their peers'.

Studying at Sister Sally's was a different kind of pain. Chinyere was constantly hovering around like a vulture waiting to land on a carcass. The boys resented this and one day they told Sister Sally to order Chinyere to study in her bedroom when they were in the house. This worked well for all of them and no textbooks ever got missing again.

The first term holiday came with James bringing home his usual perfect report card. Monday, well, he tried his best. Like he explained to his mother, grandmother and real brothers he had had a pass grade in his favorite subjects, and had failed only in French and Mathematics, which were compulsory subjects anyway. Chinyere was first in her class, and Enanga was among the first ten. Nkongho's children had done well. She bought drinks to celebrate and the party went on deep into the night forcing the tears Mami Nzelle had been repressing all this while to pour out in broad day light. Not all her children had done well. One had failed so badly that Mr. Esag was threatening to send her to live with his parents in the village and learn how to farm.

But next door the cheers and laughter went on and on as each working child tried to pull their weight by passing rounds of drinks. First, it was Glory; then it was Jacob and Simon, and finally Sally brought two crates of assorted drinks. That night they all slept in the house. Even Sally and the older boys who had their own places now stayed the night to seal Nkongho's children's success. But the following morning life returned to normal as they went about their daily business. Mami Nzelle and her friends gathered on her verandah to crack their egusi. There was a lot she could not understand. Casting an eye in the direction of Nkongho's house, she spat on the ground. "Ah say-eh, Mami Patricia, when do those children really study-eh?" She asked Mrs. Sama.

"I don't really know too-oh. That James like that who is always running to the market to buy something, hmmm!"

"You see, Chinyere, I can understand. She sleeps in Sally's house. So I can understand how she can be clever. Big, empty house even my dullest Lucy will pass too with flying colors."

Mrs. Sama sighed. "My problem is that James. Since when did he become so clever? That boy like that can make like play like that and become a doctor someday-oh!"

"Ah, ah, you too!" Mami Nzelle chided. "How can you think of such a thing? He is just a boy whose luck is shining now. Just wait."

"You people are talking, what about that small Enanga too?" The other woman remarked. "Look at her own sister, Glory."

"Ah, is that somebody? When we talk of people you mention that one too? All Glory has is water in that her fat coconut head," Mami Nzelle said.

"But there's no lie about it; she can make a good wife," the other woman added.

"I agree with you."

"Me, too. But what kind of man is stupid enough to marry her?" Mami Nzelle wondered. They burst out laughing.
"She has been with every man who is not her relative."
"Hey, Mami Nzelle, don't say a thing like that. She hasn't been with my man; yours perhaps, but not mine."
Mami took offense. "Did you catch them together?"
"No."
"Then don't say a thing like that. My man is not that stupid."
"So it is mine who is stupid-eh?"
"Ah, ah, you too Mami Patricia. Can't you take a joke?"
As they argued back and forth the other woman remained quiet, then suddenly coughed alerting them of her presence. "I actually caught her with my man," she said simply.
"What?"
"Mami Nzelle, Mami Patricia, why do you two act surprise like that? Who do you think bought her that new Dutch Wax she wore last Sunday? I saw it in my room and the next thing I see it on her."
"Your man bought her that? I thought it was the beer manager, you know," Mrs. Sama said.
"No, it is my foolish husband whose own wife ties Cicam to njangis."
That killed the conversation, for none of them wore imported wax or laces to njangi on a regular basis. Occasionally, yes; but not every week!

That academic year went swiftly as usual and soon it was time for James and Monday to write G.C.E. It all went well and as to be expected James got all ten of his papers with a series of "A"s and "B"s. Monday got four "B"s. It was a great day at the Elates, even though Monday cried his heart out for not having all six papers. There was so much chaos in the house that for the first time Mr. Esag wondered—sincerely—what was really going on next door. When Mami Nzelle explained what had happened he strolled over and gave some money to the boys. His own son had just six papers: three "A"s and three "B"s. When he was done congratulating them he went back home and beat up his son. "Damn fool," he screamed at him. "Look at your friend in a calaboat house. He got ten papers! A child of a husbandless woman for that matter! Eh? And you were a boarding student."
"Papa, her mother is a nurse. She gave him brain pills. I actually saw some in their house," the child explained.

"Yes, Papa boy, she gives them brain pills. I actually saw them in their house too," Mami Nzelle concurred.

"You shut up your dirty mouth. If my son has water in his head it is because he inherited your empty coconut head. And you stupid child, you there, go get your book and start reading this instant. You are going to write all the other two papers that you failed. You get in for eight and end up with six? Eh?" He sighed. "You must get all eight before I can be satisfied, you hear?"

"Yes, Papa."

Mami Nzelle ran after her son. "Papa, do not cry; you've done your best. See, take this money and go and celebrate with your friends." The boy was unsure about that.

"Don't worry, I'll cover for you. Just go and enjoy like all your friends who have passed." He thanked her and left before his father could suspect anything.

"Mami Nzelle, you are where?" He thundered from the parlor where he sat poking his teeth with a tooth pick. She hurried in. "Remember that it is Nzelle's turn. I don't want that Chinyere to beat her the way that her Anambra brother did our son, you hear?"

"Yes, sir."

"Okay, go tell your daughter to get ready. No child without a father will beat my child. I won't take it. So listen well because if it happens again I will bundle you all and send to the village to work farm."

Mami nodded. Thinking the session was over she started to leave the room.

"Where do you think you are going?" He bellowed. She stopped where she was.

"Did I ask you to leave? Eh, you this woman whose children can't even pass exams well?" She stood still and waited for his permission to leave the room. He said nothing of the sort, instead he ran his angry eyes over her frightened body several times then sighed resignedly. "Look at you. Get out of my sight; some lazy thing." She walked away happy to be free. Mr. Esag spent the next hour swearing and sighing and when he came out his eyes were so red that one would have been tempted to conclude that he had actually been shedding tears. Only men do not do such things. They laughed; they gloated; they grinned; they grunted but they did not cry, not even when their child has been beaten by a child who had no father. And in this manner Mr. Esag hopped on to his Suziki and rode off. Mami Nzelle seized this opportunity to join the party next door.

The very next day Nkongho took James to visit Ngozi and her family. When she arrived at Ngozi's place the younger woman began laughing. She had already heard the news

"I told you so," Sister Nkongho.

"Your son, James has done wonders."
"I told you so-eh, Sister. Don't joke with us-oh,"
"I know."
Ngozi brought out a present for James tied in a wrapper. A big bundle containing a Nigerian history book, some stockfish and yams, which she dragged after her. James thanked her. Nkongho hugged her and thanked her several times.
"Wetin man go do now? The child has done well; we have to thank God."
"Isn't that so?"
As they walked back home Ngozi stopped every now and then to introduce Kalu to friends and neighbors. It was the same response—a handshake and an exclamation.
James felt so proud of himself as people showered him with gifts and attention. Nkongho too got carried away in the moment and lost track of time. It was such a perfect day until they arrived home and discovered Monday missing.

No one knew what had happened. He failed to show up that night and subsequent nights for a whole week. Nkongho wanted to call the Police but Aunty advised against it. She said she had seen the look that Jerome had had in his eyes before he had run away. It was the same look Monday had. They were a bunch of greedy males who were unable to appreciate what they had, she assured Nkongho.
"That your son, Monday is like his Uncle. Useless and selfish," she added.
Nkongho sighed, James cleared his throat.
"What now, my son?"
"Aunty, Monday is not useless-oh. I don't really know what his problem is. But he has a problem." All eyes turned to the boy as they ate their garri and okro soup that evening for supper.
"Who asked your opinion?" Glory said, irritated that James dared to contradict their grandmother. But before he could reply Jacob interrupted. "How do you know?"
James remained silent this time. Simon shrugged his shoulders, "Is there someone who doesn't have problems? If he wants let him carry his own on his head."
"Sister," James addressed his mother directly, "Monday wants to be a big man someday. He doesn't want to sell in the market too."
Jacob sighed. "Who was going to make him join us? Look at me trouble-oh. He can go to school until he becomes a doctor if he wants. What is my own there?"
"No, you don't understand. He wants to be a boarding student next time. But with four papers I don't really know if it will be possible."

Glory laughed out loud, "Is that all? I can arrange it like that if he wants. I know people."
"Can you?"
"Of course. Is it not a government high school that you people will be going to now?"
"Yes, Sister." He cleared his throat, then coughed and cleared his throat again. Nkongho looked at him.
"James, is there something else? If there is tell us now."
"No, Sister."
"Tell us because if anything happens to your brother we shall blame it on you."
James' hands began to tremble. He stood up to leave.
"James?"
"Okay, brother Jacob, he told his friends that he would be crossing the borders to join his father. Brother Jacob, I swear that is all I know."
They were all stunned.
"We shall hear something!" Glory put in. "His father liked him so much why didn't he take him along when he was leaving the country years and years ago? Eh?" She covered her mouth in shocking disbelief. "If Sister Nkongho didn't tell you people then I will. He sneaked away just like your father too, James. Hmm! There's something definitely wrong with that Monday!"
"Glory, stop it at once. What about you? Is something not wrong with your own head?"
"Sister, I just think the boy is too selfish. He is running away from responsibilities. We have helped to train him. Two more years and he'll be ready for university, so that he can come out a big man and start helping with Enanga and Cata too. What does he do? He runs off to search for a man who doesn't even know whether he is alive or not. And you people don't want me to complain?" She got up and washed her hands. "He's your son; what's my business there even."
All was calm for a minute. Then Jacob coughed. Simon stood up to leave. Chinyere panicked. "Brother, you people should not go yet. Aunty, say something, ah beg you." The grandmother laughed. "Just give him time, he'll come right back to this house that he is running away from."
"Really?" Nkongho asked nervously.
"Of course, Epo. Forget him and eat your food in peace." She smirked and added, "A child always comes back to the mother; take it from me."
"Aunty, I don't know-oh?"
"Look at Sally's Elsie? Has her David not written that he would be coming soon? My daughter, let your Monday go. Don't give yourself high blood."

Mami Nzelle told her friends that Monday had run away but she didn't know where to. Mrs. Sama was shocked. She pushed her tray of egusi aside and pondered this for the moment. How could a child do such a thing to the mother? Her friends wondered too. The other woman who now had a baby girl sighed. "My sisters, even small children these days have sense now. Who doesn't want a good life?"
"Ah, ah, you too, Mami baby! How can a child want a good life?" Mrs. Sama replied.
"Boh, you don't know-oh. Three of such have showed up at my house. They said their mothers sent them."
"Weh, ashia. How do you manage?" Mami Nzelle consoled.
"How does a housewife manage?" Mami baby said in a flat tone.
"I still think Monday is doing the wrong thing," Mrs. Sama said.
"I feel he needs his father," Mami Nzelle fired back. "Look at Glory," she went on, "she is like a loose woman. If she had a father do you think she will be like that?"
"What about Elsie?"
"Ah, that one! See what happened to her when she came here."
"That was just her bad luck."
"No. She needed some discipline."
"See, Mami Nzelle, I am the one who beats those children. I am the one who tells them not to keep bad company. What does their father know? He comes home, eats and goes out to chase his women; then comes back and starts snoring beer all over the place."
"It is your bad luck, Mami Patricia. It is Mr. Esag who beats them, not me. I shout and insult."
"And when does he beat them?"
"When he is at home. Just leave me alone."

In her room late at night, Nkongho wished her son luck before going to bed. She tossed on the bed several times and each time she would bump into her mother. Aunty sighed.
"Epo, I've told you not to worry yourself."
"Aunty, I just can't. You know how that country is."
Aunty sighed again. "Okay, just remember that his uncle is there somewhere."
"That's true, Sister. Ah beg, let someone sleep in peace," Glory groaned from her side of the room.

"All right-oh, I hear you people," Nkongho said. But when they had all drifted to sleep she went out and sat on the verandah all by herself with a wrapper around her bosom. It was there that she felt free to let the tears she had been holding back flow freely.

She wept and wept and slept there only to be awakened early the next morning by Mr. Esag who was returning home from somewhere. She hurried in and quickly lay on the bed beside her mother and began snoring loudly.

"Epo, I'm your mother. You can cry in my presence, you hear?" Aunty whispered to her. "Don't sleep outside again like someone without a house. We have not reached that stage yet." At this Aunty too burst into tears. She sobbed for a long time thinking about her entire life before she could stop. Nkongho joined her and they wept together like they had never done before, pausing only to blow their noses. It was not long before Enanga and Catherine began moaning too. Glory slept on pretending not to hear the sad tune that was being produced by the womenfolk with whom she shared the room. She shut her eyes tight and wrapped herself well in the old faded sheet that she used as a cover. Finally, she too burst into tears and only stopped when the neighbors had begun gathering to see what was happening in the termite-infested house that harbored a bunch of sufferers. When Nkongho left for work that morning Aunty went over to Sally's and spent the entire day there on her comfortable couch. A drop of beer did not touch her lips. Just what if her grandson didn't find what he was looking for? At that moment her greatest anxiety was not fear of Monday being killed, as one would expect, but fear of whom he was going to seek out. She beamed at the thought of her own son, Jerome coming to the rescue—the only nice thing he would have ever done for the Elates.

By the end of August when it was clear that Monday was not coming back James sought admission into high school only for himself. He not only got admitted into the school of his choice, but was the first to be allocated space in the dormitory. The day he was packing out of the room he had shared with all his brothers a tear rolled down his cheek and he wondered where Monday really was. He wrote a letter to his mother thanking her for all she had done. In it he included a message for everyone. Chinyere, he wrote should continue to take her studies seriously; he said it was his wish that Enanga should stop playing too much like a boy. To Sister Glory, he pleaded that she found someone and marry, so they would have a normal life for a change. Sister Glory laughed at this as she read the letter to her mother and grandmother. But Nkongho didn't find it funny.

"So?"
"So, what?"
"Do what your small brother says."
"So I become like Mami Nzelle? Not me. Just look how they turned out."
"And me? Really, Glory, what is the difference between me and them?"
"What of Sister Sally?" Glory fired back. "She looks nice like that, is there something wrong with that?"
"I'm not saying that there's anything wrong with her. But true, true, between you and me, why is Elsie not proud of her?"
"Who says? Besides, we are not ashamed of you, Sister. Elsie has her own problems."
Nkongho shook her head to the contrary. "Glory, I'm telling you now; you want to be happy, you do the right thing."
Aunty coughed.
"But Epo, children with rich men would not hurt at all," she joked.
Glory nodded. "Aunty, you are so right."
Nkongho gave up. That night she sobbed her eyes out again as she prayed that God should give a husband to at least one of her female children. Did their family not deserve social recognition too? Weh! It was a long night as she sobbed in there while her daughter, Glory laughed coquettishly on the verandah with one of her male admirers. She was enjoying her youth so much it didn't matter whether she was doing the right thing or not. All that mattered at that moment was that she had food, drink, good health and a man she could always dump. The right thing was for book people like Chinyere who worried too much, Glory had concluded long ago. Let her just enjoy her life, na.

Chapter 10

Glory enjoyed her youth too much and a year or two later she started spitting again. This time she couldn't fool anyone; after all she was a grown woman. So she had to announce to the family that she was full with child. By whom? Sister Nkongho dared to ask. By the beer manager, Glory said. The one she had been hanging out with more often than the others for some time now. She said they planned to get married. This was wonderful news. It pleased Aunty so much that she told Chinyere that her road had finally been fixed. There was a glimmer of hope after all, and Nkongho felt relieved that at least one of her daughters would be getting married. She thanked her good fortune again and went on with her life. The boys did not hear the good news until Glory began to show. Jacob was pleased. He said, at least their family was not cursed, as he had earlier believed. He planned a small celebration for that weekend that never held, for Glory was too tired to sit with people.

"My sister, so when be the marriage, na?" He asked later.

Glory shrugged her shoulders.

"Hmm! You mean to tell me say you don't know exactly when your oga go marry you? This one is news to me. Why you fool us so-eh?"

"Glory?"

"Sister, leave me alone."

"Yes, Epo leave her alone. She has tried."

"Okay, whatever the case, hurry and marry him let everybody drink water in this house."

"I say, leave her alone," Aunty hushed her daughter. "Now, you Glory, go and tell that your man to either marry you soon or he'll pay for major damages caused, you hear?"
"Eh, eh, Aunty?"
Simon walked in looking upset.
"What now?"
"Sister Glory, really, how can you do such a thing to us again now? You, a free woman for that matter. Look at Sister Sally, have you ever seen her getting in the family way?"
"Just go with your own bad luck."
"Your own bad luck is more than mine," he retorted. This was too much for Glory, who began tumbling things in search for a missile to aim at him. Simon dodged. She aimed, he dodged. "Make God punish you, bad luck child," she screamed after him as he made for the door.
"At least, I will not marry a miserable woman like you," he replied and disappeared just in time before a text book landed where he was standing.
"Glory, are you out of your mind? Eh? Was he the one who sent you to get pregnant?"
"Sister, you people should leave me alone. That man is going to marry me. How many times do you want me to say this?"
"Okay, we hear you and we are waiting for the day that he will come and tell us himself."

They waited and waited but he never said a word about marriage, even though he was constantly there to take Glory out for a ride to go eat stockfish or bush beef. Aunty and Sally soon gave up and started making a bill for damages caused. Sally said it should be twice the amount because Glory had actually completed secondary school and deserved better. It was just the right thing to do, she explained to Aunty who nodded in agreement. They later showed the estimate to Nkongho who tossed it away and told them to back off.
"See, Aunty, this one will marry Glory whether he likes it or not. He must. No more paying for damages. That's too easy for these rich men."
"And if he refuses to marry her? Eh?" Sally asked, thinking about her own experiences with Simon. Nkongho shook her head. "He has no choice in the matter. Whether he signs a paper or not, my daughter will move into his house. Glory will not end up like me—no way!"
Aunty sighed. "You were foolish, Epo. Glory is not; that is the difference. My own plan is that he will pay for damages caused and we shall still find a way of

making Glory enter his house." She looked at the other women smiling. "That's my plan and I think it is a fine one."
Sally nodded in agreement.
"And you, Epo?"
"Okay, if you put it that way. But I don't think we should tell Glory this time."
They gave the man three months to make his intentions clear or else...

Some months later he came, bringing two bottles of Schnapps, a bottle of brandy, and a crate of beer to knock on Glory's door. Nkongho and her children all dressed up, sat in a circle as they waited eagerly for him to declare his love for their kin in front of the family. Sally sat at a corner constantly wiping a tear or two from her eyes. She wondered how Elsie's knock door had gone. She had received a letter announcing her daughter's engagement to a medical student in Yaounde, but Simon hadn't bothered to invite her to the occasion. It was only after the court wedding that Elsie and her husband had stopped by briefly to visit with her.

Nkongho's future son-in-law declared his intentions. He would be marrying Glory when the time was right, he said proudly, bending forward to touch her protruding belly. "Let's drink to that."
Everyone in the room grabbed their bottles and the merry making took off full scale. Aunty went out and invited all the neighbors to join in the festivity.
"Drink as you like, my in-law will buy some more, no be so?"
"Of course, Moyo. Simon, go bring more crates of assorted from Sally's Bar De Nuit."
The suitor bought more drinks but had to leave early he said. An urgent business he must attend to. Nobody cared as they drank and ate pieces of fried meat or fish Sally had wisely brought for the occasion. The feasting went on for a whole week with Glory missing out on work on every one of those days. But on Saturday morning Nkongho was awakened by a loud knock on the door. She heard Enanga asking who it was and Catherine saying it was a strange woman who was dressed in rich lace—not door blind lace, the little girl had stressed. Nkongho jumped out of her bed and quickly put something on. The woman, who wasn't much older than Glory smiled at her. She smiled back. "And who are you?" she asked.
"Can I just come in?" the woman wasted no time. She forced her way in shoving Nkongho from the doorway and finding a chair to sit down.
"So who are you?"

The woman hesitated, noticing Enanga, Catherine and Chinyere standing in the room with no intention of leaving. She sighed then threw her head on another side of the room. Sighed again and stared at the three girls.

"That one like that over there," she said pointing at Chinyere, "is she Glory?" Realizing her mistake she laughed hysterically. "Of course, she cannot be. Glory is pregnant."

"Yes, we all know that," Aunty replied, forcing her way between the girls in to the center of the parlor. "And who be you?" She asked as she slumped to the chair next to the woman. "Glory has gone to work."

"Okay, I am her mbanya, you know. The madam in the house," she announced gently but confidently the way people who knew they were on the right side of society's moral code did. Chinyere placed a hand over her mouth to restrain herself from calling her a liar. She cleared her throat. "Is he really married?"

"Yes, my sister. For five years now."

Aunty and Nkongho exchanged glances. On the verandah, Mami Nzelle exclaimed in disbelief. "We shall see something in this Krammer Street!"

"What will Nkongho's children not bring to us?" Mrs. Sama added.

The woman paused and momentarily looked toward the door.

"Who are those women out there?"

"Don't mind them."

Chinyere opened the door and ordered them to leave before she taught them a lesson. Mami Nzelle hesitated. Chinyere picked a stone and threw at her window. The glass shattered into many pieces. This angered Mami Nzelle so much she shoved the child away."

"Don't you do that again," Chinyere warned her.

"I will do what I want." She pushed the child's head.

"I am warning you to not touch me-oh."

"Warn me all you care, but if you play I will report you to the police and they will lock you up."

Chinyere spat on the ground just below the verandah. "I tire women like you who don't have shame."

Mami Nzelle laughed. Chinyere slammed the door in her face.

"You want to see my marriage certificate?" the woman in rich lace asked Nkongho who was still too stunned to believe the story. She pulled out a certified true copy from her leather hand bag and handed it over to her. "You see, I'm not lying."

Nkongho passed it around for the others to see. The woman began smiling again. "I don't mind him seeing her if it makes him happy, but he can never bring her into my house." She said this with such poise that Nkongho wondered out loud. "Is my Glory not good enough for his house or what?"
"Oh no, no." The woman shook her head to the contrary. "He can rent her own house if he wants."
"I see," Nkongho mumbled. At that point Chinyere left the parlor. There was a moment of silence then Aunty spoke. "So what do you want us to do now? Glory is already full with his child, you know?"
The woman nodded. "And my man likes her, I think." She attempted a wry smile. "You know I can take the child when it stops sucking. I will take good care of the baby, just like my own."
Aunty fumbled in her seat and finally pulled herself up from the bottom the weak springs on the cushioned chair had taken her. Her eyes reddened as she gaped at this rich pretty face that was telling them what they should do with their own flesh and blood. "Madam, we don't dash our children. We raise them up ourselves, you hear? You small child sitting there with your red lips, and gold earrings and whatever," she looked over the younger woman from head to toes; "what do you know about raising another woman's child? We should dash you our child and you will bring her up like your own. Hmm, bad luck go follow you!"
"Aunty, leave it like that. She is only a child herself. She doesn't know what she's saying," Nkongho pleaded.
"Child, my foot," Chinyere shouted from the room.
"You stop talking like that Chinyere."
"Sister, I will say what I like," Chinyere replied as she walked back into the room. "It's women like you who take somebody's child and maltreat." She addressed the woman directly. The woman shook her head and smiled sadly. "No, I'm not that kind of woman. See, I like children but God just did not give me one of my own."
"Then go pray hard enough for HIM to listen to you."
"Chinyere!" Aunty and Sister Nkongho screamed at her. Nkongho apologized for her daughter's behavior. "She is confused, you know."
The woman stood up to leave. "Mami," she addressed Aunty, "I am not a bad person. Believe me, she can keep the child if she wants."
"My child, I believe you. She will keep her child." Aunty snorted.

Glory was told as soon as she returned home from work that day. She cried a bit, swore a lot and laughed like a mad woman. But he is the only man that 'I have ever liked,' she told her mother. "He likes you too," Sister assured her. The words did no good to Glory who refused to have supper that evening. Instead, she drank bottle upon bottle of beer until she was hauled out to bed by her mother and Sister Sally. It rained heavily that night and by day break all the dirt had been washed away. But Glory would not come out to breathe the clean fresh air. She sent Enanga to announce at her office that she was ill.

She still would not eat and kept saying they should go bring the father of her unborn child. Aunty did not know what to do. Ignoring Glory's request, she prepared pepper soup and forced the pregnant woman to eat. Glory pushed the bowl away and insisted that they should bring the man to see her. Nkongho sent for him and he came running, wondering if she was having a miscarriage. She was not, she told him, but was glad he had finally come after one whole long week.

"Then what is the matter?" he asked as patiently as he could.

"Nothing," she said. "Just my waist." He massaged it gently.

"Does that make it feel better?"

"Yes, but my head too. It aches all the time."

Fear gripped him. "Are you sure the baby is all right?"

"I don't know anymore. But the doctor says I may lose it if I am not careful. Bills, bills, I don't know what I will do again."

He quickly wrote a check and placed on the bed beside her. "Anything you want, don't hesitate. Your health is my concern," he rambled on.

"I know. Another thing, I've not eaten since yesterday. I want chicken. No, chuku chuku beef; no, fish."

"All right, I will leave some cash with Aunty to buy you any type of food that you want. Weh, my Glory, don't fall ill-oh, my sweetie."

"I hear you."

"Just be strong. You know, first pregnancies are always the most difficult. Be brave."

"I hear you, Papa."

He hung around her until she had gobbled up all her pepper soup before he left. Aunty thanked him for his kindness and shut the door behind him.

"Glory, he is a good man."

"Yes, Aunty. I am really sick too."

"Be strong like he says. I think if you want he can dump that one in the house for you."

"Perhaps."

"But beware! Don't dash your child to him. I forbid you."

Another week later Glory sent a note to the man asking for a fridge. Without asking her why he bought it. He also bought her a gas cooker and new set of chairs. They rearranged the parlor to make room for all these new things. It was getting too crowded even for the Elates. Then one day *he* came in and said he had bought the plank house for *his* Glory. They will have to break down some walls and create more room for *his sweetie*. Aunty burst into tears. This was not happening. A man actually liked her own flesh and blood and was willing to show it! Weh! A man liking her own flesh and blood like that? Hmm! This was truly news to her and Nkongho. She felt so proud of her granddaughter that she would not stop singing her praises. Glory was a woman who knew what she wanted, not like Nkongho, her stupid mother who had been fooled by a white man's cook and a washer man. She left out Jacob, Simon and Monday's father completely—a one time Personnel Supervisor at pamol.

"What about Mola Peter? You liked him too, na?" Nkongho asked.

"Of course, I didn't know any better. He walks like a black white man looking clean in his well ironed khaki, and eating bread and butter all the time."

"Whoosh! I hear that he and his wife and children are really suffering now," Sally said.

"What did you expect of a man who thought one could live on bread alone?"

"Aunty, he showed promise at the time."

"No, he thought he was better because he worked for a Europian." She chuckled. "He forgot that he was only the man's cook! Nkongho, a cook!" She laughed harder.

"He was really better."

"He was not."

"Ah, you people should leave me with this talk about Mola. Glory doesn't even care whether he exists or not," Sally brushed them off.

"How true!" Aunty concurred.

Across the street, Mami Nzelle sat on the verandah unusually quiet with a white bandage wrapped around her left eye where her husband mistakenly hit her last night. She sat there contemplating what she would fix for lunch for her family. She had not seen Mami baby for almost a month, since the woman's husband had thrown her belongings out on the street that she should go back to her parents. Her only fault is not giving the man's child a special kind of food.

Mami Nzelle sat there with her lastborn, a stubborn little boy whom Mr. Esag swore did not resemble him at all. Not even one bit. She sighed as she reflected on her life. Not too far from where she was, Glory sat on their own verandah eating from an expensive breakable bowl. Mami Nzelle sighed. "Wonders shall never end."

"Boh, how na?" She heard Mrs. Sama from behind the house.

"Over here-oh, Mami Patricia. The usual place." She moved over to create more room on the mat for her friend.

"What happened to your eye, na?" Mami Patricia asked, feigning surprise. Mami Nzelle sighed. "As if you don't know. You heard me crying last night, what did you think was happening?"

"Enjoyment, na."

"Yes, I was enjoying."

Mami Patricia sat down and placed her egusi tray on her lap.

"Weh, Mami Nzelle! See, when Patron is slapping you hide your face. That's what I do. I show him other parts of my body, not my face. Now the world will know that he has beaten you."

"You are really funny. Don't the world know about Nkongho and her children? Are they not happy? Ah beg, leave me let me drink water."

"All right, at least, he didn't throw you out on to the street the way they did to Mami baby."

Mami Nzelle chuckled. "He can't. Who will cook for him? Who will wash his clothes? Look at Mami baby's husband; see how he is suffering alone in that his big, block house. Girl friends don't work for men. They enjoy with them." She laughed. "Do you know that two of those children she was feeding have run away?"

"Eh, is that true?"

"Of course, don't pretend. Mami Baby left and there was no one there to make them even garri to drink. Yes, they went back where they all had come from."

"Hmm! This life is really funny."

"I know, my sister."

They saw Nkongho, Aunty and Sally crossing the road to their house.

"Hmm! Lucky woman, that Nkongho so. Do you know that that man has bought the house for Glory?"

"Iyaka-eh! Tell me something."

"Mami Patricia, that Glory like that, her own luck is something else. When a man likes her, he really likes her. But the trouble is that she can never be a wife."

"Why do you say so? She is still quite young."

"Men don't like wives that way. It is too dangerous."

"But that man has asked her hand for marriage, we were all there, na?"

"Yes, he did but only because he cannot have her."

"I do not understand."
"Why did he sign monogamy with his first wife?"
"It doesn't really matter. He can still marry her if he really wants, and of course, if she presses hard. Boh, he likes her; let's face it."
"So?"
"Let him marry her and put her in her own house."
"Not Glory. She owns herself and makes her own decisions."
"Then she'll never marry, na." Mami Patricia said in frustration.
"What's your problem there? She likes her life, leave her alone."
"Why should she like that kind of a life, eh? Why?"
"Because...ah, what's my own there even?"
Both women sighed and dropped the topic.

The very next day these two women sat again on that same verandah, even though it had rained all night and continued to drizzle. As they were bickering over something, they saw this filthy person heading toward Nkongho's house. He was drenched to the core with sharp edges poking out of his rib cage. He stumbled onto the side verandah, pulled off his heavy sweater and squeezed water off his limp T-shirt then stepped back into the rain to rinse some mud off his body. He disappeared. The women took their eyes away from him and searched for something more interesting. What had they not seen on Krammer Street? Had they not seen drunken men enjoying mud like pigs? But their eyes kept shifting back to the lone figure, for Nkongho's door was shut. They were too exhausted to guess who it could be.
And the youth was too lanky to be Nkongho's child. Mami Nzelle concluded he was a beggar.
"You know mad people come in all forms."
"My sister, can you imagine that it is women that actually give birth to such people? Look at that one in the rain with his shirt off, suffer is written all over his body. And so young! Young bone skeleton." She was touched by the pathetic figure.
"Ah, ah you too, why feel sorry for such people? You think he is in his right senses? No. I bet you he has smoked too much banga and can no longer feel pain. Save your sympathies, boh."
"Weh! Fine boy who would have grown up to be someone's husband!"
"My sister, isn't that the thing? I feel sorry but for the woman that brought him in to this world. What a loss!"
"I know. Poor thing."

They were still feeling sorry for this 'unstable' youth when someone screamed in Nkongho's house. Mami Nzelle jumped from her seat spilling all her egusi on the wet ground. "Weh!" she exclaimed. Mrs. Sama smiled and gave a look at her friend that said I told you so, for that poor thing they had wasted their sympathies on was Monday himself. He had actually retuned home to his mother where he belonged.

"What?"

"Mami Nzelle, he came back home," Mrs. Sama cheered, with eyes glittering with the motherly pride that had sustained her in her children's father's house for so long.

"Wonders shall never end."

"What did you expect? That his father will just accept him for the child he is. No, they don't do that. When you are somebody, eh-heh!"

"Even then Mami Patricia, is a child not a child?"

Mrs. Sama chuckled. "Just wait until those your children start failing.

Mami Nzelle sighed. She knew what her friend meant only too well but she didn't want to be bothered by it at that moment. So like the concerned neighbors who wanted to hear what had happened to the boy they went over to Nkongho's to not only see with their own eyes, but also hear too. But before the boy could say anything Chinyere slammed the front door shut and closed all the two windows. The neighbors still would not budge. They waited and waited for something to happen. When nothing happened for a while, one by one they began to leave. Mami Nzelle loitered around until she saw them open the door for James and his big brothers who had just heard the news.

"So what happened?" Jacob thundered as soon as he sat down on the new comfortable couch.

"Leave the boy alone," Nkongho rebuked.

"No. Monday, how is our father? Tell us."

"He is well," he mumbled.

"Again?"

"He is well."

"That's good news. So why did you run away like that? Were we not giving you enough to eat in our poor home?"

"Yes, you people did."

"Were you not in school?"

"Yes."

"What is it then that you wanted, eh you this cocoyam head?"

Tears streamed down Monday's wet face.

"Did he give you money? If so, divide it among the three of us."
"He didn't give me anything."
"So why did you go there again? Answer me before you continue crying like a baby."
"Jacob, leave the child alone."
Simon who was quiet all this while cleared his throat and stared at his brother.
"How far is that place where our Papa and his people live?"
All eyes turned toward him.
"If you dare, Simon; if you dare go find him, I will kill you with my bare hands."
"Ah, ah brother Jacob!"
That evening they ate a sumptuous meal of chicken that the beer manager had ordered for them to celebrate Monday's arrival and life went back to normal.

CHAPTER 11

September came by very fast and the rains poured like hell washing away the filth from Krammer Street and bringing in more filth from elsewhere. Still, September did not come fast enough for Chinyere who now called herself Daisy. It was the English name her grandmother had given her at birth and she felt it was time she went by it. After all, she was in high school now.

Early mornings, she would put on her well-ironed navy blue, pleated skirt and light, blue shirt and bounce along the dirty road in front of their house until she joined her friends on the other side of the street that had tar. Her black cut shoes, the ones recommended by the school officials, she packed neatly away and flip flopped her way toward CCAS, the highest school of learning in K Town. Her school supplies, she protected delicately in another part of the bag, zipping it close so nothing would ruin it. She was Daisy, and tried to be the flower she had blossomed into. Rich men in fancy cars smiled at her; so did taxi drivers and petty traders on bicycles. Even pedestrians—those men who cannot even afford a spoke for a bicycle whistled at her. This business of looking good, na wa-oh! She would laugh out loud and toss her micro braids on the side of her powdered face and tried bouncing onward. But this was hard on flip-flops. Then she would catch even chauffeurs of big men eyeing at her and slowing down to offer her a ride. Daisy would sigh and brush them off. BAD LUCK men weh their own no dey sef. Others whistled and waved. Her chest would swell sometimes from anger until she saw the kind of man she believed should dare look at her! It was always like that. Every morning. Daisy hung close to her books though. No be that book give *them* money? She always rationalized in her mind. No be that book they takam pass *we*? She relished the thought of beating them at it. Some day, just maybe!

She had never forgotten Sister Sally's story. Wasn't her only crime that she had not tried hard enough to pass that G.C.E O/levels like clever boys did? Daisy had crushed it like nothing and now she planned to break a record in CCAS. Perhaps then her road would be really open, so that only correct people would even dare approach her for a date. Twenty-four months or less and this would happen. She would show people that she was really an Elate. Bush thing weh dem think say we are all off the road!! She was almost certain her brains would fetch her a director of something some day and a wife of somebody bigger than the director she aspired to be. No church rat in her future at all! All these thoughts ran through her head daily as she waddled in the mud puddle struggling to bounce as well on her way to school.

Brother James now calling himself Kalu, the name his father had given him at birth, was special. Thinking of him brought a smile on Daisy's face. Her special brother was now one step away from the university. It was all Aunty ever boasted about these days as they awaited the birth of Sister Glory's child. But the beer manager had postponed the wedding date again. This time he said, "we shall see; not long from now" like a man who lacked for money. One Saturday, he stopped by to announce that he wanted to make a wedding that would shake K Town; and one like that needed more than money. He was working on it. So we shall see, remained the verdict.

Glory said okay and demanded a weekly allowance. He agreed. Every week, he brought a wad of crisp thousand francs notes and a leg of dried bush meat. He would grin all that day touching the stomach of the mother to be of his child fondly, feeling the baby's heart beat. He would be a Papa soon. He could not wait. Papa, the word rang in his ears and he would dip into his "cunning" pocket and bring out another wad of notes. The big man was indeed happy. Glory could not complain. What else did she want? Soon, she too started wearing rich laces and tying Dutch Wax, Java Print, George wrapper like the madam in the house. This pleased her brothers very much. That was a sign of true love. No be so a man who likes a woman get for take care of her? They marveled at the attention and gifts the big man showered on Glory. It was true love; they declared at dinnertime, night after night hoping that just one day Glory would push harder to become his real madam!

The more stuff the big man provided to Glory, the more she realized that she would never dash them her child as his madam had proposed. Why should she? See what had happened to her kid brother, Monday.

As for Monday too, the troublemaker finally enrolled in lower sixth form with Chinyere. Oops! Daisy. What else could he do? He was officially stuck with the Elates. He hated September so much and watched the rains pour nonstop on some days forcing him to miss classes. It would pour heavily on some days and paused intermittently for the people on Krammer Street to clear the debris from wherever. Some did; some like Nkongho didn't care. The debris would always come back. Why bother? And so the time passed.

With each rainstorm or thunderstorm that hit Krammer Street, the Elate's plank house trembled. They could feel the foundation shaking beneath them. But then it would stop as suddenly as it had occurred. The white wash that graced the external walls had long chipped away. It was a bare house at the mercy of the elements. It did not fear though, standing there all these years like an exposed wound that would never heal. What did the people on Krammer Street do to deserve this? Mami Nzelle and her crew had ceased to ask.

In front of the square, termite infested building stood a heap of sand. It kept mounting as the father of Glory's unborn child anticipated the arrival of *his child*. At the back of the house bricklayers were busy molding bricks non-stop. And for the first time since she started making and raising children Nkongho heaved in a sigh of relief. Let the rains damage her foundation; she would rebuild it as always.

"At least, we've found our own plum tree," she mumbled.

Aunty laughed.

"Even if it is only for now, na?"

"Yes, Epo," she paused. "True, true, that your Glory is something-oh! I tell you."

"She's trying her own best, Aunty."

"She has done well. Better than you and Sally."

"Aunty, you too."

They laughed as they crossed the gutter to join Sally in her Bar de Nuit. Life was looking good for these mothers.

978-0-595-38266-
0-595-38266-5

Printed in the United States
57421LVS00001B/97-111